Fasten Your Seat Belts!

"Dave?" Amanda cried, pounding his shoulder. "Dave—why are you doing that? Stop! Stop it—please!"

Dave continued to sway, his expression blank, his eyes unblinking.

"Dave—please! Please!" Amanda shrieked helplessly.

Suddenly Dave pitched forward.

His forehead slammed hard against the steering wheel.

"Dave!" Amanda screamed.

She cradled his head in her hands and tried to pull him up.

But when she saw his face, she let go.

Books by R. L. Stine

Fear Street

THE NEW GIRL
THE SURPRISE PARTY
THE OVERNIGHT
MISSING
THE WRONG NUMBER
THE SLEEPWALKER
HAUNTED
HALLOWEEN PARTY
THE STEPSISTER
SKI WEEKEND
THE FIRE GAME
LIGHTS OUT
THE SECRET BEDROOM
THE KNIFE
PROM QUEEN
FIRST DATE
THE BEST FRIEND
THE CHEATER
SUNBURN
THE NEW BOY
THE DARE
BAD DREAMS
DOUBLE DATE
THE THRILL CLUB
ONE EVIL SUMMER

The Fear Street Saga

THE BETRAYAL
THE SECRET
THE BURNING

Fear Street Cheerleaders

THE FIRST EVIL
THE SECOND EVIL
THE THIRD EVIL

Fear Street Super Chillers

PARTY SUMMER
SILENT NIGHT
GOODNIGHT KISS
BROKEN HEARTS
SILENT NIGHT 2
THE DEAD LIFEGUARD

Other Novels

HOW I BROKE UP WITH ERNIE
PHONE CALLS
CURTAINS
BROKEN DATE

Available from ARCHWAY Paperbacks

One Evil Summer

A Parachute Press Book

AN ARCHWAY PAPERBACK
Published by POCKET BOOKS
New York   London   Toronto   Sydney   Tokyo   Singapore

This book is a work of fiction. Names, characters, places and incidents are products of the author's imagination or are used fictitiously. Any resemblance to actual events or locales or persons, living or dead, is entirely coincidental.

AN ARCHWAY PAPERBACK *Original*

An Archway Paperback published by
POCKET BOOKS, a division of Simon & Schuster Inc.
1230 Avenue of the Americas, New York, NY 10020

Copyright © 1994 by Parachute Press, Inc.

All rights reserved, including the right to reproduce this book or portions thereof in any form whatsoever. For information address Pocket Books, 1230 Avenue of the Americas, New York, NY 10020

ISBN: 0-671-78596-6

First Archway Paperback printing July 1994

10 9 8 7 6 5 4 3 2 1

FEAR STREET is a registered trademark of Parachute Press, Inc.

AN ARCHWAY PAPERBACK and colophon are registered trademarks of Simon & Schuster Inc.

Cover art by Bill Schmidt

Printed in the U.S.A.

IL 7+

One Evil
Summer

chapter

1

One Evil Word

Amanda Conklin rolled over in bed. She opened her eyes and stretched slowly.

Did I leave my tank suit on the line last night? she wondered. Yes. I'll wear my two-piece instead. I hope it's early enough to take a swim before summer school.

She turned toward her bed table to read the clock. If I get up right now, I can probably get to the pool in time, she thought, her mind still hazy.

"Huh?" Amanda blinked hard. The table wasn't there. Neither was her bedroom.

Her eyes darted wildly. The moment she saw the gray cement ceiling, she remembered where she was.

And everything that had happened.

Grabbing hold of her rough sheet, she yanked it over her head and rolled herself into a ball. Go away, world. Just go away! she thought.

A piney, antiseptic odor crept under the sheet. Amanda felt as if the smell had implanted itself in her nose forever.

Metal bedsprings screeched. The other girls in the room began getting up.

Good morning, fellow psychopaths. Amanda laughed bitterly to herself.

Clack, clack, clack.

Amanda recognized the sound of footsteps on the hard floor. She'd quickly learned that only the guards made that much noise. Everyone else shuffled along in soft green slippers. In the wing for "psychologically disturbed offenders" they were permitted nothing hard or sharp. Not even a shoe.

Of course, Amanda knew not to call these harsh, noisy women "guards."

She was supposed to call them by their names. Ms. Macbain. Mrs. Garcia.

Amanda called them guards.

"Up, Conklin! Let's go!" barked Mrs. Garcia, a fat woman with short brown hair and beady, dark eyes.

Amanda knew she had no choice but to push down the sheet. The rules at the Maplewood Juvenile Detention Center were strict.

A worn gray towel hung over the metal frame of Amanda's bed. She grabbed it as she stepped into her official Maplewood Juvenile Detention Center

2

green paper slippers. Rubbing sleep from her eyes, she folded her arms over her official-issue, pocketless green nightgown.

"In line," commanded Mrs. Garcia. The girls lined up by the door. Amanda followed them down the cold mustard yellow hall to the bathrooms.

As she walked, she glanced out the barred windows. What a rainstorm! It looked as if someone were tossing buckets of water against the glass. A sudden crack of thunder made Amanda jump.

I'd do anything to be out in that storm, she thought miserably. Freedom—even the freedom to be wet and shivering—would be better than this.

Anything would be better than this.

They stopped outside the bathroom entrance. They were allowed to go in four at a time. When Amanda's turn came, she went inside with three sullen-looking girls. Other "psychologically disturbed offenders" like herself.

I probably look as bad as they do, thought Amanda. She glanced at the others from the corners of her dark eyes. All us psycho-offenders have a certain look.

Inside the harshly lit bathroom, Amanda splashed water on her face. She stared at her reflection in the mirror.

Not good, Amanda, she silently told her reflection. You're a disaster! Her large brown eyes had dark circles under them. Her suntan had turned yellow—the same sickly color as the walls.

And what's happened to my perm? she wondered, tugging on a listless, drooping curl. Her hair had flopped dead in just three days.

That's how long I've been in this nightmare place, she told herself. Just three days. It could be three years.

Amanda sighed. Might as well try to get used to it. I'll be here a long time.

She remembered overhearing her lawyer when he told her parents that she couldn't go home with them. "Murder is an extremely serious offense," he said.

"No kidding!" Amanda laughed to herself as she brushed her chestnut brown hair.

The girl at the next sink glanced up at her sharply.

Amanda turned away. Great, I'm talking to myself now. I really am wacky. Maybe I *do* belong here, she added.

"Hurry up in there," Ms. Macbain, a big woman with cakey makeup, shouted into the doorway. "Conklin, you have an appointment with Dr. Miller right after breakfast. Put a move on."

Amanda cringed. Not another session with Dr. Miller! The day before he'd asked her so many questions, her head throbbed. What had happened? What had she been thinking? How had she been feeling?

Amanda didn't want to talk to him anymore. Why keep talking when it could all be boiled down to one word? One evil word . . .

Chrissy!

chapter
2
Chrissy

"**S**o long, Fear Street. Seahaven here we come!" Amanda cheered as her father pulled the car out of the driveway. She watched her house grow smaller and smaller as the family drove away.

Amanda fished a yellow hair scrunchy from the pocket of her khaki shorts and pulled her long brown ponytail through it. Then she kicked off her tan leather sandals and pushed up the long sleeves of her lightweight yellow T-shirt. She settled back into her seat and smiled at the kids to the right of her. Her brother Kyle was eight, and her sister Merry was three.

In minutes the seat felt hot and sticky. "Can you turn on the air conditioner?" Amanda asked her parents.

5

"It's on," Mr. Conklin called back.

"Well, we can't feel it!" Kyle whined.

"I'm cold!" Merry complained. She liked to be different.

Amanda gazed out at the old houses bathed in shade. Fear Street looked so normal in the daytime, she thought. But at night . . .

She shuddered. Why am I thinking about this now? We're getting away from here!

Amanda was happy she wouldn't be stuck in Shadyside for the summer. She and her family would be at the seaside town of Seahaven. Her parents had rented a house not far from the ocean. It would be a working vacation for them.

Her father, a lawyer in the public defender's office, defended people too poor to hire a lawyer. He'd asked to have no trials for the summer so he could catch up on a mountain of paperwork.

Mrs. Conklin was a journalist. Her latest assignment was a magazine article entitled "New Pressures on Today's Young People." It would be about the stress of being young in the modern world. She planned to finish the article in Seahaven.

As their car merged onto the highway, Mrs. Conklin turned toward the backseat. "Amanda?" she asked thoughtfully. "What would you say is your greatest source of stress?"

Oh, no! Amanda groaned silently. Please don't start with the questions already! I can't take it! Have mercy!

"Well?" Mrs. Conklin prodded as she pushed her dark blunt-cut hair back into a leather headband. "I know there are a lot of stresses in your life. But which do you feel is the greatest?" Sometimes Amanda felt like a living test-case for her mother's articles.

"Sitting next to these two!" Amanda answered wryly, nodding toward Kyle and Merry in her car seat. At the moment Merry was happily smearing the grape jelly half of her peanut butter and jelly sandwich on Kyle's shirt.

"Hey—stop!" Kyle complained.

Merry just giggled, her wispy brown curls bobbing in delight as she swiped at Kyle's straight blond hair with her bread. "I bru*th*ing your hair!" she lisped gleefully.

"I said *stop!*" Kyle screamed.

"See what I mean?" cried Amanda.

"Don't *you* complain," Kyle grumbled. "I'm the one squished in the middle, getting all yucked up."

Mrs. Conklin reached back and gently pushed Merry's hands away. Then she attempted to wipe jelly off Kyle's shirt.

Merry reached into the back of the compact station wagon and yanked the cloth off the cage of the family's canaries. Amanda had named them Salt and Pepper. One had a white speck at the end of its yellow tail and the other's wing tips were flecked with black.

With the cloth off, the birds immediately began

to warble. Amanda's orange tabby cat, Mr. Jinx, started meowing from his carrier wedged on the floor between Amanda and Kyle.

"Come on, Jinxie," said Amanda as she gently lifted the heavy cat from the carrier and settled him on her lap. Mr. Jinx licked her hand and curled into a contented ball.

"Seriously, Amanda, what do you find most stressful in your life?" Mrs. Conklin asked again.

I hate these questions! Amanda replied silently. But she knew her mother wouldn't give up until she got a real answer.

"Algebra," Amanda replied.

Mrs. Conklin's smile drooped. Her large dark eyes lost their excited gleam.

Why did I say that? Amanda asked herself. That was really brilliant! I had to go remind them that I failed Algebra II.

And they'd gone an entire morning without mentioning it!

Oh, well, thought Amanda, scratching Mr. Jinx behind the ears. There's nothing I can do about it now. Still, I feel bad that Mom and Dad have to hire someone to take care of Kyle and Merry while they work. I *did* promise I'd do it. But I can't since I'll be imprisoned in summer school at Seahaven High for half the day.

"I really hope someone good answers my ad for a mother's helper in the *Seahaven Daily*," Mrs. Conklin fretted, turning forward in her seat. "My article has to be turned in by the end of July, and I'm already behind."

Amanda sighed and slumped low in her seat. I had to go open my big mouth.

"We'll find someone terrific," Mr. Conklin said to his wife as the air-conditioning ruffled his thinning blond hair. "Don't worry."

Two hours later Amanda spotted the Seahaven exit. They turned off the highway and then drove another half hour along a narrow, twisting road, Old Sea Road.

As the little beach town of Seahaven came into view, Amanda pressed close to the glass. "What a cute town," she commented as they passed art galleries, restaurants with awnings, sports stores, and one old-fashioned general store.

"Look at that!" cried Kyle, pointing.

Amanda saw a life-size statue of a brown bear with a fish in his paw. It stood on a plot of grass in the middle of a traffic circle.

"I hear the fishing is excellent here," Mr. Conklin commented.

They drove around the circle and out the other side. Amanda realized they were climbing high above the ocean. "Is our house on a mountain or something?" she asked.

"It's just on a hill, but about five minutes away are gorgeous bluffs that overlook the ocean," her father replied.

Finally her father turned into a community of

summer houses surrounded by woods. Off to the side of a narrow road stood their house, a modern but rustic structure with a peaked roof and gray wood shingles.

"It's cool!" declared Amanda, climbing out of the car with Mr. Jinx in her arms.

Merry and Kyle hurried out behind her. Immediately they began running around on the small front lawn.

Mr. Conklin unlocked the door to the house and Amanda followed him in. "Cool," she repeated.

She approved of everything—the high ceilings with two skylights flooding light into the modern living room, the large sliding-glass door that took up most of the back wall. She even liked the blue-and white-striped curtains at either side of the glass doors.

Excited and happy, Amanda pushed the glass door aside and stepped out onto the wooden deck. Below it, a square swimming pool glistened in the leaf-dappled sunlight.

"Awesome!" Amanda murmured.

She listened. She heard only the soft, steady rustling of the leaves and the muffled crash of the waves from the ocean on the other side of the sloping woods.

Smiling, Amanda hurried back outside to help her dad.

Kyle and Merry almost knocked her over. "Whoa, you guys!" She laughed. They were so

excited, they didn't seem to know—or care—
where they were going.

She continued on down the gravel driveway. "I'll
take that," Amanda offered as her father pulled her
flowered duffel bag from the open hatch.

"There's even a little skiff with an outboard
motor that comes with the house," said Mr.
Conklin. "We can try it out later."

Amanda lugged the heavy bag into the house.
Her mother stood in the triangular-shaped white
kitchen off the front hall. "There's not a thing to eat
here," she said to Amanda. "I guess we'd better go
into town for supplies."

"Me come wif you!" cried Merry, tugging on her
mother's white pants.

Mrs. Conklin scooped her up. "Okay."

"I'm coming too," shouted Kyle from the living
room. "I want to see that awesome bear again."

"I am *not* getting into the backseat with those
two again!" cried Amanda. "I'll stay."

"All right," Mrs. Conklin agreed as she ushered
Merry, Kyle, and Mr. Conklin out the door. "We
might stop to see the Bakers while we're in town.
They're staying at the Beachside Inn. If you need
us, call there."

"I won't need you," replied Amanda with a
wave.

A chirp made Amanda turn toward the birds'
cage. "I guess you'd like a nice sunny spot," she
told them, picking up the cage. Amanda placed it

11

on a table that stood behind the couch. "You guys should be happy there."

As if in reply, the birds began singing.

Mr. Jinx swished his tail back and forth. "You behave, Jinx," Amanda said with a smile.

Amanda headed upstairs to her bedroom and began to unpack. She turned on the radio and danced as she piled her things into the small drawers. Then she heard a knock on the door.

Who can it be?

Amanda made her way downstairs to the front door.

On the other side of the screen stood an extremely pretty girl. Amanda guessed she was about seventeen. Her eyes were so blue that Amanda wondered if she wore tinted contact lenses. The color of the girl's long, straight hair reminded Amanda of the silk on the inside of fresh corn on the cob.

She was slim and athletic looking with long legs. She had on a white halter top and wide, soft blue slacks.

"Hi," the girl said in a lightly husky voice—the kind of voice Amanda longed for. "I'm here about the ad."

"The ad?"

"The mother's helper job," the girl said.

"Oh, *that* ad!" Amanda exclaimed. "Sure. Come on in."

"I'm Chrissy Minor," the girl said as she entered.

"I saw the ad and thought it would be just right for me."

"That's great," said Amanda. "Unfortunately, my parents went out for a while."

"Oh, wow." Chrissy's face fell. "I scheduled another interview at one o'clock." She shrugged. "Oh, well, if the other people hire me, then I'll figure I wasn't meant to have this job. If they don't, I'll check back."

"Wait," said Amanda. She knew her mom and dad were desperate to find someone right away. "My parents might be at the Beachside Inn. I could call there and check to see if . . ."

Amanda's voice trailed off. Chrissy's expression had changed. Her blue eyes narrowed as she stared past Amanda into the room.

Hissssssssssss!

Amanda turned toward the sound.

Mr. Jinx was standing on the couch with his claws out, his back arched, his orange- and white-striped hair on end. She could see his fangs as he hissed again.

"I'm so sorry," Amanda apologized. She scooped up Mr. Jinx and petted him. "He's never done that before."

"Maybe I should go." Chrissy was already moving toward the door.

"No—please!" Amanda begged, holding Jinx firmly. "Wait a minute. Let me call my parents. I know they'll want to talk to you."

13

Chrissy checked her delicate gold watch. "I suppose I can wait a few minutes," she agreed.

Amanda hurried into the kitchen. She closed the door and set the cat gently on the floor. "What's gotten *into* you?" she scolded him mildly. "Now, behave yourself."

Amanda called local information to get the number of the Beachside Inn. A few seconds later her parents were on the line.

"We'll be right there," said Mrs. Conklin eagerly. "Ten minutes, tops. Don't let her leave!"

Amanda hung up. She turned in time to see the end of Mr. Jinx's striped tail as he slipped through the crack where the door had opened. "Hey— Jinx!" she called.

Amanda heard Mr. Jinx hiss again.

A shrill, frightening sound. She had never heard the cat hiss like that.

She froze in the doorway when she caught sight of Chrissy.

The girl's shoulders hunched up. Her blue eyes narrowed again, and their whites had taken on a faint yellowish glow.

"Oh." Amanda let out a low cry of surprise as Chrissy bared her teeth—and hissed back at Mr. Jinx.

chapter

3

An Evil Secret

Chrissy let out another animal hiss, an inhuman sound.

With a terrified yowling shriek Mr. Jinx raced past Amanda back into the kitchen.

Amanda bent down, picked up the cat, and petted him to soothe him. "You got a taste of your own medicine, didn't you?"

Mr. Jinx nuzzled his head into the crook of Amanda's arm. His hair was still standing on end. Amanda had never seen him like this.

"My parents will be right back," Amanda called out to Chrissy. "You can sit down."

Amanda got a bowl of water for Mr. Jinx and petted him until he calmed down. A few minutes later, she heard the front door open and her parents greet Chrissy. Kyle suddenly burst into the kitchen with Merry at his heels. "Is she the new baby-sitter?" he demanded.

Amanda gazed out the open door to the living room where her parents were interviewing Chrissy. "I don't know yet," she told Kyle.

But, peering through the door, she decided that things looked good for Chrissy.

Mr. Conklin sat forward on the couch, his hands folded. His blue eyes were warm with approval as he spoke to Chrissy.

Beside him, Mrs. Conklin sat back, nodding her agreement with Chrissy's every word. As Amanda watched from the kitchen, she could tell her parents were completely taken with Chrissy.

"Hey, can you make me lunch? I'm starving," Kyle asked Amanda.

Amanda grabbed a can of tuna from the grocery bag he had brought in and opened it. She began making sandwiches for Kyle and Merry. She continued watching the interview as she worked.

"That looks totally gross!" Kyle complained as he swiveled around on one of the high wooden stools by the breakfast bar. "Watch what you're doing. You're slopping the tuna all over."

"Totally groa*th,*" Merry echoed, swiveling on the stool beside him.

"Shh!" said Amanda. "I want to hear what Chrissy is saying."

"I live with my aunt outside of town," Chrissy was explaining to the Conklins. "But her daughter, my cousin, just returned from college, and the house seems a little small with the three of us there. A live-in job would solve the problem for me until Eloise goes back to college in the fall."

"Have you done this sort of work before?" Mrs. Conklin asked.

"Oh, yes. I've been a mother's helper for the last two summers."

"How old are you?" asked Mr. Conklin.

"Seventeen."

"Do you have any references from your other jobs?" Amanda heard her mother ask.

Chrissy dug into the large flowered canvas pocketbook she carried and pulled out a typed sheet of paper in a clear plastic cover. "Here's my résumé," she said. "The references are on the bottom."

"Let me go call one of these," Mrs. Conklin said as she got up. "I'll be just a moment." She went into the kitchen and shut the door behind her.

"Are you going to hire her?" Kyle asked immediately.

"Do you want me to?" Mrs. Conklin asked.

"I don't need a baby-sitter," Kyle said. "But she'd be good for Merry."

"What do you think of her, Amanda?" Mrs. Conklin questioned.

"I don't know," Amanda admitted. "But you should have seen the way Jinx hissed at her. And she *hissed* back at him. Her face got really strange when she did it. She bared her teeth and everything!"

"Oh, I guess she has a good sense of humor," Mrs. Conklin said, laughing. "I like her."

"Sense of humor? I don't know, Mom," said Amanda. She couldn't forget the expression on Chrissy's face.

"Hire her," said Kyle. "What a babe!"

"Kyle! Where'd you hear talk like that?" Mrs. Conklin scolded, punching in the numbers from Chrissy's sheet.

Even from several feet away, Amanda could hear the irritating buzz of the busy signal. "I'll try this other number," said Mrs. Conklin.

No answer at the second number.

"Hire her anyway, Mom," Kyle urged. "You always say you can tell about people."

"Yes, usually I am a pretty good judge of people," Mrs. Conklin answered. "And she seems perfect. I'd hate her to take that other job."

"You can't hire her without checking her references," Amanda whispered.

"Well, I'll check them later, but I don't want to lose her now."

"Mom, that's totally irresponsible!" Amanda insisted.

"Amanda, it was totally irresponsible of you to fail algebra," her mother replied sharply. "If that hadn't happened, I wouldn't have to be making this decision."

Amanda couldn't argue. How could she stop her mother from hiring a mother's helper when it was her fault they needed one?

Amanda heard laughter in the living room. She turned and saw Chrissy leaning toward Mr. Conklin in a friendly, confidential way. "And you should have seen how your cat hissed at me," Chrissy was saying as if it had been a big joke to her.

"I cleaned up a mousetrap this morning for Aunt Lorraine," Chrissy continued. "Your cat must have smelled the mouse on me. Animals have such a sensitive sense of smell."

"They do," Mr. Conklin agreed. "Especially Jinx. He can smell tuna inside the can!"

He and Chrissy shared a laugh.

Amanda found herself feeling foolish. Perhaps she had made too big a deal out of the way Mr. Jinx had reacted.

She went out to the living room. Folding her arms, Amanda perched on the arm of the couch. "I couldn't reach either of your references," Mrs. Conklin told Chrissy.

"Oh, you couldn't? That's a shame," Chrissy replied. "I don't think they'd have anything bad to say about me, though."

"No, I'm sure they wouldn't," Mr. Conklin agreed, smiling warmly. He took off his glasses. Amanda knew what that meant. He was finished talking about whatever he'd been discussing.

"If you want the job, Chrissy, it's yours," said Mrs. Conklin, smiling warmly.

Chrissy beamed at them. "Terrific! Oh, I'm so glad!"

"Kyle, Merry, come meet Chrissy," Mrs. Conklin called into the kitchen.

Shyly, the kids came out, first Kyle, then a tiptoeing Merry.

Chrissy stood up and bent forward toward them. "Hi, guys," she greeted them, her whispery voice rich and friendly. "I'm so happy to meet you two."

Merry clung to Kyle, but she beamed happily at Chrissy.

"You're not really going to be baby-sitting me," Kyle informed her, squaring his narrow shoulders.

"Oh, I knew that. Of course not," said Chrissy. "But I could use your help."

"Sure. No problem," Kyle told her. "If you need to know anything, just ask me."

"Thank you, Kyle," said Chrissy. "I'll do that."

Amanda rolled her eyes and held back her laughter. Chrissy had won over Kyle—easily.

"Amanda, I'm happy that we'll be spending the summer together," said Chrissy. "I think we'll have a great time."

"Yeah. I'm sure we will." Amanda had meant to make her reply more friendly. But the words slipped out halfheartedly.

"I packed and brought my suitcase—just in case," Chrissy told the Conklins. "I'll be right back."

Amanda didn't watch Chrissy leave the room. Her attention had been drawn to the birdcage. To the silence.

Salt and Pepper had stopped singing. Usually, they sang nonstop all day. At least one or the other trilled merrily.

Now they were silent.

Amanda walked over to the cage and checked to see if they were sleeping. They weren't. They were huddled together on the perch.

"Hey—check out the birds!" Amanda cried.

Turning, she realized she was talking to the air. Everyone had gone outside with Chrissy.

Amanda bent down to the birds. "Sing," she whispered, softly pinging the bars with her fingers to get the birds going.

As if waking from a trance, Pepper began to chirp. Salt soon joined in.

"Weird," Amanda muttered. Then she hurried outside to join the others.

A few minutes later they trooped upstairs to show Chrissy her room. "I'll put you here next to Kyle and Merry," Mrs. Conklin said as Mr. Conklin set the suitcase down and left. "Why don't you unpack and get into your bathing suit? We'll meet you down by the pool."

"Great," Chrissy said cheerfully. "A house with a pool! Am I lucky or what?"

Mrs. Conklin left with Kyle and Merry, but Amanda hovered in the doorway, leaning against the side.

She watched Chrissy swing her old suitcase onto

the twin bed. As the suitcase bounced, its metal clasp sprung open, sending clothing tumbling to the floor.

Amanda stooped to pick up the clothes. As she lifted a blue cotton sweater, newspaper clippings fell out. "What are those?" she asked, raising her eyes to Chrissy.

The sweet smile disappeared from Chrissy's face. "Nothing," she snapped, scooping up the clippings.

Chrissy whirled away from Amanda, the clippings clutched to her chest.

Amanda climbed to her feet. What was Chrissy hiding?

Chrissy turned around sharply. "Here," she said, holding an article out to Amanda.

Amanda took it. It was beginning to yellow. The date on the top was from two years before. The headline read "Lilith Minor Still in Coma."

Silently, Amanda read the article.

Lilith Minor, 15, remains in a coma after her admittance to St. Andrews Hospital last week. Doctors at St. Andrews hold out little hope for her recovery.

According to doctors, the teenager, who inhaled a nearly lethal dose of carbon monoxide, may have incurred brain damage. If she comes out of her coma, doctors say she might suffer from any number of possible brain disorders.

"How sad," said Amanda. "Is she a relative of yours?"

"My twin sister," Chrissy replied casually.

"What happened to her?" Amanda demanded.

Chrissy stared at the yellowing article. "Lilith's still in a coma," Chrissy answered.

"I'm so sorry," Amanda said softly.

Without warning, Chrissy grabbed hold of Amanda's wrist.

She squeezed the wrist tightly, so tightly it hurt.

"Don't be sorry for her," Chrissy rasped. "Lilith is evil!"

23

chapter

4

Problem in the Pool

"**D**o you want a ride?" Mrs. Conklin offered Amanda on Monday. She was on her way to her first day of summer school at Seahaven High.

"No, thanks, I found a bike in the shed. I'll take that." Amanda hurried out onto the deck and ran down the wooden steps to the shed beside the pool.

She could see Chrissy heading down the path that ran through the woods to the beach. Kyle and Merry danced happily along beside her.

Chrissy looked terrific in a gauzy white beach shirt, the tan of her long legs set off by the white of the shirt.

Chrissy waved and Amanda waved back. "Good luck," Chrissy called.

Over the weekend her family had fallen completely in love with Chrissy. It's all right, I guess, Amanda thought as she opened the shed. They act sort of goofy around her, but as long as everyone is happy, I suppose it's okay.

Amanda found the old bike and walked it around to the front of the house. Riding along the narrow, curving road into Seahaven, she thought about Chrissy.

Why had Chrissy said her sister was evil? What had Lilith done?

The narrow road widened gradually. Soon Amanda was rolling rapidly as the downward slope of the hill sped her into the town of Seahaven. She braked as she entered the traffic roundabout, and circled the bear with the fish.

Seahaven High was in the middle of town. Amanda parked her bike in a rack out front and went in. In the lobby a sign directed her to Room Ten.

There were only eight or nine other kids in the class. Amanda took a seat toward the back.

"It's a beautiful summer day and none of you wants to be here," the teacher, Ms. Taylor, said. She was a young woman with very short blond hair and a lightly freckled face. "But we're here anyway, so let's make the best of it."

Amanda liked Ms. Taylor immediately. She was a tremendous improvement over old prune-faced Mr. Runyon, who had taught algebra back at Shadyside High

Amanda glanced around. Sitting next to her was a tall boy with wavy brown hair, broad shoulders, and large hazel eyes. Cute, Amanda noted.

He seemed to sense her eyes on him and turned. He smiled at her.

Very cute, she decided. When Ms. Taylor called the roll, Amanda discovered that his name was Dave Malone.

"Grab a partner and work on the first three problems on page ten," Ms. Taylor instructed. With a flash of white teeth, Dave smiled at Amanda and slid his desk closer to hers.

It was hard to concentrate on the work while sitting so close to such a great-looking guy. Luckily, Dave understood the problems and solved them easily.

"Why are you in summer school?" Amanda asked. "You know this stuff."

"This x, y, z stuff, yeah," he said with a smile. "It's the later stuff, the tangents and arcs and things, that messes me up."

"You're ahead of me, then," Amanda admitted. "I got lost right here at a equals x. I've even forgotten what I used to know from freshman year."

"This part isn't hard," Dave said. "Here, think of it like this. . . ." With pencil and paper, Dave explained the problems in a way that made sense to Amanda.

"I wish you'd been my teacher," Amanda said

26

after successfully completing a problem. "Then maybe I wouldn't be sitting here right now."

"But then we wouldn't have met," Dave said lightly.

Amanda suddenly felt shy. "No, I guess not."

After class Amanda and Dave walked out of the school together. "Are you from Seahaven?" Amanda asked.

Dave nodded. "Lived here all my life."

"Do you know anyone named Chrissy Minor?"

"Nope."

"Do you know an old woman named Lorraine, maybe Lorraine Minor? She has a daughter named Eloise, who goes to college."

Dave thought a moment, then shook his head. "Don't know them."

"But doesn't Seahaven have a small winter population?" Amanda asked. "I'd think you'd know just about everyone who lives here."

"I thought I did," said Dave. "Why do you want to know?"

Amanda shrugged. "I'm just being nosy, I guess. My parents hired a mother's helper—Chrissy Minor—and I was curious about her."

"Don't know her," said Dave. "Maybe she just moved here or something."

"Maybe," Amanda agreed doubtfully.

"Is she nice?" Dave asked.

Amanda didn't really know what to say. "Yeah. She's okay. But—well—I don't know. This is going to sound really dumb."

"Go ahead," Dave urged, smiling. "I major in dumb."

"Well," said Amanda reluctantly, "I don't trust her—because my cat hates her. Is that stupid or what?"

"Pretty stupid," Dave agreed. He laughed. "No. Wait. I'm only kidding. I mean, I think animals are real good judges of character. They sense stuff and don't have to be polite the way we do."

"Do you really think so?" Amanda asked.

"Yeah," Dave said as they walked. "I had this dog once. He always growled at this one kid I knew from school. It turned out that the kid was a klepto, always stealing stuff. After he swiped my favorite video game, I listened to the dog."

"Tell that to my parents," Amanda said. "They think Chrissy is Miss Perfect."

Amanda had reached her bike. She climbed on and said goodbye. "See you tomorrow!"

On the way home, she thought about what Dave had said about animals. Then she started thinking about Dave.

He *was* really cute!

When she reached the house, Amanda leaned the bike against the front. She went inside. "Mom?" she called.

No answer.

"Merry? Kyle?"

Silence.

Amanda shoved the glass door open and hurried out onto the deck.

She looked down at the pool. Her heart slammed into her throat.

Merry!

Merry floating in the center of the pool.

Her eyes closed.

Her wispy hair spread like a fan around her face.

Merry!

Frozen in horror, a single thought screamed into Amanda's head.

Merry can't swim!

chapter

5

Jinxed

"*Merry—no!*"

Had that scream really come from Amanda?

Her feet pumping hard, Amanda raced down the deck stairs to the pool.

"Merry! Merry! Please—Merry!"

She dove in, fully clothed. Thrashing wildly, she swam to her sister.

When she was halfway there, Amanda sensed something under the water, a moving shape.

Huh? What was down there?

With a surge and a splash, the thing blocked her path, rolled up in front of her.

"Oh!" Forgetting that she was underwater, Amanda cried out in fear. Choking and sputtering, she quickly realized she was face-to-face with Chrissy!

It was Chrissy. Chrissy under the water with her.

"What's going on?" Amanda demanded breathlessly as soon as she surfaced.

"You tell me," Chrissy shot back. *"You're* the one in the pool with all your clothes on!"

Brushing water from her eyes, Amanda saw that Merry was hanging on to Chrissy's arm. "I was floating," Merry said proudly.

"Huh?" Amanda cried, not recovered from her shock. Her heart still raced in her chest. She struggled to slow her breathing.

"I was teaching her to float," Chrissy explained. "I was under the water, holding her up, when you dove in like a lunatic."

At that moment Mrs. Conklin came running out to the pool with Kyle close behind. "What's going on?" she cried. "What's all the shouting?"

Mrs. Conklin stared at Amanda, then at Chrissy. "Uh—no problem, Mom," Amanda said. "Really."

Mrs. Conklin frowned as Amanda dragged herself out of the water, her shorts and T-shirt soaked. "Amanda, couldn't you find a bathing suit?"

Kyle laughed. He thought it was a riot.

Leaving a trail of water across the deck, Amanda joined her mother. "You look like a geek," Kyle chortled.

Amanda glared at him. Mrs. Conklin jerked her thumb toward the pool. "Kyle, go join Chrissy. Amanda and I need to talk."

"Amanda, what is the problem here?" Mrs.

Conklin demanded when they were alone at the end of the deck.

"I thought—I thought that Merry was drowning," Amanda replied, avoiding her mother's eyes. "I saw her just floating there and I swam out to save her. Only she really was floating. Chrissy was teaching her to float."

Mrs. Conklin's face softened when she heard the explanation. She brushed a strand of wet hair from Amanda's forehead. "You must have been so scared," she said softly.

"Mom, I have a bad feeling about Chrissy," Amanda blurted out.

"Amanda, are you still worrying about the cat?" her mother asked.

"No. Not that," Amanda whispered. "The birds too. The birds don't sing when Chrissy is around."

"Amanda," her mother said, shaking her head. "Please—let's be reasonable. What's really bothering you?"

"I don't know, Mom. It's just a *feeling*. And this guy I met in school, he never heard of her. And he's from around here. Chrissy doesn't live in Seahaven."

"She said she lives with her aunt *outside* of town," Mrs. Conklin reminded Amanda.

"Maybe you should check out the address she gave you, see if it exists," Amanda suggested.

"I'm not going to spy on her," Mrs. Conklin said.

"Did you check out her references yet?"

"I keep calling, but the one line is always busy

and the other doesn't answer," Amanda's mother replied.

"Don't you think that's weird?" Amanda asked.

"No," her mother replied. "One family probably has one or more teenagers who monopolize the phone. And the other is away on vacation. I don't find it strange at all. I'll get through eventually, and when I do I'm confident the people will tell me good things about Chrissy. I think she's delightful."

"Did you know she has a sister in a coma?" said Amanda. "She told me her sister was evil."

"That's not what she told me," said Mrs. Conklin. "She's very upset and worried about her sister. We should be kind to Chrissy. She's been through a hard time. She told me her parents were killed in a car accident. Her sister was the only family she had, and now she's in a coma."

"Then why did she tell me Lilith was evil?" Amanda insisted.

"Amanda, are you sure that's what she said?"

"Positive. And she said it in a really creepy way too."

Mrs. Conklin shook her head wearily. "I think your imagination is playing tricks on you." After ruffling Amanda's wet hair, Mrs. Conklin made her way back into the house.

Amanda leaned against the deck railing. Down in the pool Chrissy was throwing a colorful beach ball with Kyle and Merry. The picture of happy summer fun.

Up in her room, Amanda peeled off her sticky,

wet clothes. Mr. Jinx settled on the patchwork quilt of her twin bed. Amanda scratched behind his ears. "I wish you could talk, Jinx," she said quietly. "I need you to tell me why Chrissy makes you so stressed. I need to understand."

Almost as if he understood her words, Mr. Jinx pressed his head into Amanda's hand and rubbed. "I love you too, Jinxie," Amanda said with a smile.

She pulled on tan shorts and a red and black Pearl Jam T-shirt. Then she headed for the kitchen to get a snack. Mr. Jinx trailed behind.

On the way she passed the bedroom her parents were using as an office. Her father sat in a comfortable chair, sorting through a stack of papers. His long legs were sprawled in front of him. He was so intent on his work, he didn't even look up.

Mrs. Conklin had placed her laptop on a small desk in the corner of the room. She sensed Amanda's presence and turned around, smiling quickly before returning to work.

When Amanda and Mr. Jinx passed the front door, the cat rubbed up against it. "Sure, I'll let you out," Amanda replied to his unspoken request. She opened the door, and Mr. Jinx scurried out.

Amanda continued on to the kitchen. She gazed out the window as she tore open a bag of Oreos. Chrissy, Kyle, and Merry had moved around to the front of the house.

On the small patch of front lawn to the left of the gravel drive, Chrissy and Kyle batted a shuttlecock back and forth with badminton rackets. Merry ran back and forth between them.

Popping an Oreo into her mouth, Amanda watched them absently. She was dimly aware of a silver hatchback approaching rapidly out on the road.

From the corner of her eye, she noticed Mr. Jinx as he moved up the driveway.

Amanda heard the engine of the silver car rev loudly.

She heard the squeal of tires.

"Hey—" she cried. "What's going on?"

Through the window, Amanda saw Mr. Jinx dart across the lawn.

"No!" Amanda shrieked as the silver car suddenly veered sharply.

Out of control!

It's out of control!

The roar of the car drowned out Amanda's shrill screams as it leaped onto the front lawn.

The car was heading straight for Merry and Kyle!

chapter
6

Rising Fears

*H*er hands pressed against the kitchen window, Amanda screamed as the car careened wildly, bouncing across the lawn.

It all happened in a blur.

Merry screamed.

Kyle raised his hands in front of his face.

Chrissy dove toward them.

And then all three disappeared behind the roaring car.

"Merry! Kyle!" Amanda heard the frantic shouts of her parents.

The ground seemed to tilt and sway as Amanda led her parents out the door to the front yard.

And then the ground shook as the silver car smashed hard into the Conklins' parked car.

And stopped.

Silence now.

Except for the frantic cries of Amanda's mother. "No! No! No! No!" A chant of utter terror and disbelief.

"It's all right!" Chrissy's shrill cry burst over the chant. "They're all right."

Amanda gaped, trembling, gasping for air.

Chrissy, Kyle, and Merry had dived to the ground. Now they started to pull themselves up, clinging to Chrissy, ashen and shaking.

"Thank goodness!" Mrs. Conklin sobbed. "Thank goodness you were here to save them, Chrissy!"

Kneeling down to them, she hugged her children tightly.

"Mommy, Mommy, Mommy," Merry cried, throwing herself around her mother's neck.

Amanda turned to the silver car. A young man with short blond hair climbed out slowly from the driver's side. "Are they all right?" he asked, dazed, in a quivering voice.

"What happened?" Chrissy demanded angrily.

"I—I don't know," the man stammered, shrugging. "Honestly, it was the weirdest thing!" He gazed at his car. It was smashed into the passenger side of the Conklins' station wagon.

"My car—it just started to pick up speed," the man continued shakily. "I couldn't steer it. The brakes—I pushed down hard. But they wouldn't work."

"Have you been drinking?" Mr. Conklin asked suspiciously. "If you have, I swear I'll—"

"No!" the man protested. "Not a drop. I don't drink. I—I really, I don't know what happened. I wasn't speeding. I wasn't drinking. Honest. I feel so bad. . . ." His voice trailed off. He lowered his eyes.

"We'd better call a tow truck," Amanda's father muttered, cooling down a bit. "Thank goodness no one was hurt."

As her father started toward the house, Amanda spied a familiar orange-striped tail near the front tire of the silver car.

Amanda knelt and gently slid Mr. Jinx's lifeless, bleeding body out from under the car. "Someone *was* hurt," she said softly.

Glancing up, Amanda caught Chrissy's eye. She was positive she saw a smile on the girl's lips.

No! Amanda thought. *No! Chrissy isn't smiling! She isn't!*

The smile—if it had been a smile—faded in an instant.

Amanda picked up the cat and climbed to her feet. "You're glad he's dead," she murmured bitterly to Chrissy.

"Amanda, please," said Mrs. Conklin. "We're all upset about Mr. Jinx. But don't take it out on Chrissy."

"I—I feel so terrible about your cat," said the man, shaking his head. "I didn't see him."

Amanda opened her mouth to speak, but her voice choked as tears slid down her cheeks.

Kyle stood beside her and petted Mr. Jinx's lifeless head. "Poor guy," he said sorrowfully.

Still carrying the dead cat, Amanda walked around the house toward the woods. She grabbed a spade that was leaning against the shed.

"Wait for me," called Kyle, who had come hurrying after her.

A few feet before the sloped woods let out onto the beach, Amanda spied two boulders. The large rocks stood at an angle to each other, forming a narrow opening, just wide enough for one person to squeeze through.

That's a perfect spot, Amanda decided as she began digging.

Kyle stood and watched as she pounded the rocky dirt with the dull tip of the spade.

Amanda glanced up from her work as Kyle crouched and stroked Mr. Jinx's limp body on the ground beside her. He disappeared for a few minutes and reappeared with a handful of leaves and pine branches. "This will make him a good bed," he said, placing the greenery into the hole Amanda had dug.

They laid Mr. Jinx into the hole, then covered him with more greens before shoveling the dirt over him. The surf behind them thundered steadily in Amanda's ears.

"Wasn't that weird how that car just shot up onto the lawn like that?" Amanda asked, patting down the dirt.

Kyle shrugged. "I was so scared," he confessed.

"I was trying to hit the badminton birdie. I didn't even see it coming. Did you see it?"

"Yeah, I saw it. It was just like the man said. The car suddenly had a life of its own."

"Scary," Kyle murmured.

"Yeah. Scary."

Numb. That was the only way to describe how Amanda felt.

She couldn't finish a single hot dog when the family barbecued out on the deck. She couldn't believe her sweet little cat was really gone.

After dinner she shut herself in her room and tried to concentrate on her algebra.

Sounds of laughter floated up from the living room. The others were all playing charades. Amanda's parents were desperate to get the kids' minds off what had happened that afternoon.

No one even asked Amanda to play. Amanda didn't know how to feel about that.

Maybe they wanted to give her some space, knowing she was upset about Mr. Jinx. Or had they just forgotten about her? Was Chrissy taking her place?

Unable to concentrate, Amanda shut her algebra book. Sighing, she headed down to the living room to join the others.

Standing in the hall entryway, she watched them. Everyone was so engrossed in the game, no one noticed her.

Chrissy stood in the middle of the circle. She was acting like a creature with claws. Then she placed her fingers at her temples.

"A bull!" Kyle guessed.

Chrissy shook her head no. She clawed the air again.

"Cat!" Merry guessed.

Chrissy touched her nose to signal that was the right answer. Then she snatched off Kyle's baseball cap. She tossed it on the floor, kicked off her sandals, and stepped into it.

"The Cat in the Hat!" Mrs. Conklin guessed.

"Right!" cried Chrissy gleefully.

The cat in the grave, you mean, Amanda thought bitterly.

She turned and hurried back up to her room. With a sigh, she flopped onto her bed. What a day . . .

She suddenly felt exhausted.

With the silver-gray twilight spilling into her window, Amanda drifted into a troubled sleep.

Her dreams were a garble of images and voices. At one point she dreamed Mr. Jinx was drowning in the pool. She jumped in to save him. But a giant octopus swam up from the bottom of the pool, wrapping her in his huge tentacles.

Frantically Amanda struggled to wriggle free.

No use.

Like a swimmer caught in a riptide, she felt

powerless to escape a force greater than herself. To her horror, she saw the bottom of the pool open up into vast blackness.

As if heading for home, the huge octopus plunged down into the black hole, carrying the struggling Amanda down, down, down into the endless blackness.

Amanda awoke. And sat up, confused.

I'm still dressed, she thought.

When did I fall asleep?

She stared into the darkness. What was that red glow?

It was the dial of her digital clock.

Slowly her eyes adjusted to the dark. She remembered where she was.

Not in a dark hole. In her bedroom in the summerhouse.

She listened to the quiet. The chirp of the crickets outside rose up through the silence. The red numbers of the clock told her it was twelve twenty-eight.

Amanda stood up and made her way to the window. A full pale moon shone down on her.

Amanda's stomach rumbled. Her mouth felt dry. I need a drink of water, she decided. Rubbing her eyes, she slipped out into the dark hall.

The house lay quiet. Everyone had gone to bed. Silently, Amanda moved down the hall.

As she neared Chrissy's room, she saw that the door stood open.

Had Chrissy gone out? Cautiously Amanda peered into the dark room.

Chrissy stood in a shaft of shimmery moonlight. She wore a long, sleeveless white summer nightgown.

As Amanda watched, Chrissy tossed her head back and laughed loudly.

Why does she look so tall? Amanda wondered, staring into the dark bedroom.

Are my eyes playing tricks on me?

Am I still dreaming?

Suddenly Chrissy sensed Amanda's presence and whirled around sharply.

Amanda's hand flew to her mouth.

In the pale moonlight Chrissy's face was contorted—and so evil.

Chrissy stared hard at Amanda and laughed. Joyless, scornful laughter.

Amanda wanted to turn away. But she couldn't. Something in Chrissy's gaze was holding her.

Holding her. Holding her.

So tall . . .

Why was Chrissy so tall?

And then Amanda saw.

No! She uttered a silent cry of disbelief.

No!

But it was true.

Chrissy was floating half a foot off the floor!

chapter
7

Stressed Out

Deep purple splotches floated before Amanda's eyes. Part of her wanted to sink back into the blackness. The other part was struggling hard to come fully awake.

The splotches slowly faded to gray.

The fog cleared, and she saw her father's face. Very far away. Then closer.

Closer.

"I think she's coming to," Amanda heard him say. She felt something cool on her forehead. Then her mother's worried face moved out of the gray blur.

"What happened?" Amanda asked weakly. "My head hurts. Why are you here?"

"You must have fainted," Mr. Conklin told her.

"I got up to get a glass of water and found you on the floor outside Chrissy's room."

Chrissy! The name jolted her memory.

Amanda struggled up onto her elbows. "You have to get rid of her!" she pleaded shrilly. "You have to! Please!"

"Calm down, Amanda," said Mrs. Conklin, taking her arm gently.

Amanda tossed her mother's hand off. "I *can't* calm down. Something terrible is going to happen to all of us if we don't get rid of her!"

Amanda tried to keep her voice from trembling. She knew she sounded out of control. But she couldn't help it.

They had to listen to her. They *had* to!

"Chrissy was—floating. I saw her!"

Mr. and Mrs. Conklin exchanged worried glances.

"Listen to me!" Amanda insisted. "Chrissy was floating. She was nearly a foot off the floor! Why do you think I fainted?"

Mr. Conklin rubbed Amanda's shoulder. "We don't know, hon, but we're sure that—"

"No!" Amanda cut him off. She jumped up from the floor. "Come. Come with me. You'll see for yourself."

"Amanda—stop!" her mother pleaded.

But Amanda turned toward Chrissy's room. With a shove, she pushed the door in. She turned back to see that her parents were right behind her.

Then she stepped into the bedroom. In the darkness she saw Chrissy on her side in bed.

Asleep?

"What's going on?" Chrissy lifted her head. "Is there a problem?" Her voice came out a sleep-filled whisper.

Amanda realized her entire body was trembling. "You were floating!" she shrieked. "Don't deny it! I saw you!"

"Floating?" Chrissy asked, rubbing her eyes. "Amanda, I don't understand."

This innocent act was more than Amanda could take.

"Listen, I've never imagined anything before!" she cried angrily. "And I didn't imagine this!"

Chrissy raised her eyes to Amanda's parents. "Is she joking or something?"

Amanda saw red. Something inside her snapped. She leaped at Chrissy. "Liar! Liar!" she screamed. She grabbed Chrissy's shoulders and shook them, hard.

Chrissy's mouth opened in shock.

"Liar! Liar!" Amanda cried in a shrill, high voice she had never heard before.

Abruptly she felt two strong hands pulling her off Chrissy.

Mr. Conklin grabbed Amanda around the waist and tugged her back. He held on so firmly that she couldn't break free.

"I'm sorry, Chrissy," he said. "Please, go back to sleep. I'm terribly, terribly sorry."

Chrissy was still breathing hard. She pulled herself up shakily. "Is Amanda okay? Why is she so upset? Is there anything I can do for her?"

"No. Please," Mr. Conklin insisted. "We'll handle her. She'll be okay. Try to sleep."

Amanda didn't struggle. She allowed her parents to pull her from the room.

Down the stairs. Into the living room.

Her father sat Amanda down on the living room couch, keeping a gentle but strong hold on her wrists.

A whirl of emotions swept over Amanda. Fear. Embarrassment. Anger. Desperation.

The feelings swelled—until she could bear it no longer. Then suddenly it felt as if a dam burst, and Amanda collapsed in great heaving sobs.

She bent forward, buried her face in her hands, and let the tears come.

After a while she heard someone enter the room. Glancing up, she saw Kyle, sleepily rubbing his eyes. "What's the matter with Amanda?"

Mrs. Conklin got up quickly from the couch and turned him around. "It's nothing, sweetheart. Amanda is just upset about Mr. Jinx. Go back to bed."

"I don't blame her," Kyle mumbled as he obediently stumbled back toward his bedroom.

"Maybe your mother's right," said Mr. Conklin kindly. "I think you might be in shock over what happened today. I'm still a bit shocked myself. I know how much you loved Mr. Jinx."

Amanda's sobs had begun to subside. But the mention of Mr. Jinx set her off again. She felt as if she might never stop crying.

Mrs. Conklin returned from getting Kyle back to bed. She lowered herself to the couch on the other side of Amanda. "Honey, do you feel like Chrissy is replacing you in our affections?"

"Mom—please!" Amanda said. "I can't take those questions now!"

I just want them to believe me, Amanda told herself.

I know what I saw in Chrissy's room. I *have* to make them believe me.

She wiped the tears from her face. She took several deep breaths, trying to calm herself. "Mom, Dad, have I ever fainted before?"

"No," Mrs. Conklin admitted.

"Have I ever imagined anything crazy before?"

"No," Mrs. Conklin replied softly.

"Then why would I imagine something now? And why would I faint unless I'd seen something completely terrifying?"

"Amanda," her father said thoughtfully, "you ate almost nothing at dinner. You had a hard day. You might even be coming down with something."

"You might have been sleepwalking," her mother suggested. "You probably dreamed that you saw what you think you saw, and then you went to sleep there on the floor."

"That sounds very possible," Mr. Conklin agreed.

Possible? Possible?

Was it possible that she dreamed Chrissy floating up off the floor—and fell asleep in front of her bedroom door?

Yes, Amanda reluctantly admitted to herself. It *was* possible.

A lot more possible than Chrissy floating in midair.

Maybe you're right," she gave in wearily.

Her mother shifted her weight on the couch. "You know," she started, "writing this article about stress in teenagers has been a real eye-opener for me. There are so many different pressures on kids. Perhaps you'd like to talk to a counselor or therapist."

Amanda groaned. "I'm not a kid in your article, Mom. I don't need a therapist."

Mrs. Conklin sighed. "Sometimes we all need to explore our feelings. I just finished reading a book about sleepwalking as part of the research for my article. A lot of times it means the person is really stressed."

Amanda looked to her father for help. He gazed at her thoughtfully. Then he said, "Why don't we leave this for the morning? I think the best thing for all of us right now is to get some sleep."

Amanda settled under the sheet. She still felt wide awake.

She no longer felt the urge to cry. But she

couldn't stop her mind from returning to all that happened since Chrissy had arrived.

And again she saw Chrissy, hovering, her bare feet floating nearly a foot off the floor.

Chrissy floated!

Or had she?

How can I blame my parents for not believing such an insane story? Amanda wondered. She had to admit that the sleepwalking theory made the most sense.

With the lights out, Amanda lay in bed, listening to the crickets. Even with the shade drawn, a line of white moonlight crept in the window, etching a line on the wood floor.

Amanda suddenly felt exhausted. Completely drained.

But she was afraid to sleep. She was sure she'd dream of Chrissy's contorted, laughing face. Even if it had been only a dream, it was a dream she didn't want to have again.

Finally she drifted into an uncomfortable sleep. A short sleep. When she awoke, her clock read two-fifteen.

Amanda sat up in the dark room. The sound of the crickets had stopped. Now Amanda heard other sounds.

Someone was awake and moving around the house.

Every nerve on edge, Amanda slipped out of bed. Her curiosity overpowered her fear as she crept out into the hall.

Was it Kyle? Or her parents?

She had to know.

Keeping close to the wall, Amanda crept toward Chrissy's room. Her pulse quickened as she realized the door was open.

She fought down a strong urge to run back to her room. She didn't want to know what she might see if she peered into Chrissy's room again.

Summoning her courage, she peeked into the room. Chrissy's bed was empty. The rumpled covers were illuminated by a patch of moonlight.

Amanda took a deep breath. Chrissy—where are you? Why are you up?

She followed the sounds downstairs to the kitchen. The kitchen light was on.

She saw Chrissy. Chrissy had thrown a lightweight pink robe over her nightgown. She was leaning against the kitchen counter, eating from the open bag of Oreos and gazing thoughtfully out the window.

Just a late-night cookie binge!

Amanda breathed a sigh of relief.

Happily she made her way back up the stairs to her room. She stopped outside Chrissy's room.

Whoa!

The newspaper clippings!

They were lying in the middle of Chrissy's bed.

Why didn't I notice them before? Amanda wondered. Then she saw that the moonlight had shifted a bit. The clippings had been hidden in darkness before.

I've got to see those newspaper stories, Amanda decided. I've got to find out what Chrissy didn't want me to see.

She checked back over her shoulder. Chrissy was still down in the kitchen.

This is my chance, Amanda told herself as she stepped into Chrissy's room.

What are you hiding in here, Chrissy? What?

Her heart pounding, she bent over the bed and gathered up the clippings. There were about fifteen of them.

With a trembling hand, Amanda picked up one of the news stories and read the headline, "Teenager Remains in County Hospital."

She let it drop and picked up another article.

But before she could raise it close enough to her face to read in the dim light, Amanda felt a cold hand grab the back of her neck.

chapter

8

Down in Flames

Amanda lurched away. The newspaper clippings tumbled from her hands onto the floor. She whirled around. "Chrissy!"

Chrissy didn't say a word. But her face was twisted with fury.

Amanda rubbed her neck. She could feel cold marks where Chrissy's fingers had been.

Suddenly a sharp ocean breeze swept in through Chrissy's half-open window, scattering the clippings across the floor.

Am I seeing things? Amanda wondered. Is Chrissy somehow sweeping the clippings away from me? In the pale shaft of moonlight, they sailed and tumbled toward the door.

Chrissy stepped back and stood stiffly like a pillar of rage, her clippings lying at her feet.

"Get out of my room, Amanda," she whispered, her eyes narrowing dangerously. "What's your problem, anyway? First you attack me while I'm sleeping. Then you sneak into my room."

She tossed her head as if shaking away her anger. "Whatever it is, get over it! If I ever catch you here again—"

"I—I—won't—not ever again." Fighting hard to stay calm, Amanda hurried past Chrissy, avoiding her harsh stare.

Chrissy slammed the door behind her.

Amanda froze in the hall. She wanted to run to her room and lock the door. But something stopped her.

The moonlight poured in through a skylight above her head. In the light Amanda saw that one of the clippings had been blown out into the hallway.

After snatching it up, she ran to her room. Closing the door with one hand, she flipped on the light.

Her hands trembling with excitement, Amanda stared at the clipping. The first thing she noticed was that the story was from the *Harrison County Gazette.*

Harrison County was not far from Shadyside. About a twenty-minute drive. Why was Chrissy interested in something going on in Harrison County? It was certainly a long way from Seahaven.

Like the other clipping Amanda had seen, this one was also two years old.

Her heart pounding, Amanda sat on the edge of her bed and read it.

The article told of a terrible tragedy. Mr. and Mrs. Anton Minor of Harrison County had been found dead in their beds one morning. Only their daughter, Lilith Minor, was alive. But as Chrissy had already revealed, Lilith lay in a coma with little hope for recovery.

According to the clipping, the deaths were believed to be accidental. Someone had left the family car running in the attached garage. First the garage had filled with carbon monoxide. Then the deadly fumes traveled through the heating and cooling duct system into the house. The Minors breathed the carbon monoxide while they slept. Mr. and Mrs. Minor never awoke. Lilith hadn't awakened either, according to the newspaper.

Amanda stared at the clipping, puzzled.

Why was there no mention of Chrissy in the article?

No mention of Chrissy at all.

Was Chrissy living with her aunt at the time? But why would that be?

Maybe she had just been away somewhere, Amanda thought. But didn't these news stories usually mention surviving members of a family?

It might just be a case of incomplete reporting, Amanda decided. Her father was always complaining about how reporters didn't get all the facts when covering some of the criminal cases he tried.

"Whoa!" Amanda exclaimed out loud.

Chrissy had told her mother that her parents had died in a *car* accident.

That wasn't exactly true. Why had Chrissy lied? And why wasn't she anywhere in the news story?

I have only one piece of the puzzle, Amanda told herself. I have to find out the rest somehow. The other clippings must have the information I need.

She yawned. Enough for one night.

Feeling weary, she walked to her window, pulled up the shade, and gazed out into the moonlit woods. Seahaven is so gorgeous, she thought. Everything would be so perfect if it weren't for Chrissy.

In the morning I'll find a way to get hold of those other clippings, she decided. It can't be that hard to do.

I'll find a moment when Chrissy is out with the kids. Then I'll go into her room and read them.

I'll tuck this clipping away tonight, she decided. Tomorrow I'll show it to my parents. It'll prove to them that I'm not completely crazy—that I'm not wrong about Chrissy.

Maybe Chrissy *hadn't* floated. Maybe that part was just a dream, Amanda decided.

But something about Chrissy is weird. She isn't what she pretends to be.

Amanda moved away from the window. She opened her top drawer to hide the clipping under her underwear.

Suddenly she became aware of a strange, tingling heat in her fingers. "Hey—" she cried out.

56

She gasped as the newspaper article burst into flame!

"Ow!" The white-hot flames scorched her fingertips.

Amanda flung the fiery paper across the room.

"No!" She stared in horror as the flame caught on the fringes of the striped throw rug. A line of flame shot quickly up the border of the rug.

Uttering another cry of horror, Amanda frantically grabbed her large, fluffy pillow and started beating it against the flames.

"No! No!"

As Amanda desperately pounded the flames out, she became aware of a frightening sound.

Laughter?

Who is laughing? Where is it coming from?

She glanced around the room. To her horror, Amanda slowly realized the laughter was inside her own head.

She clutched her forehead.

The sound wouldn't stop.

Such evil laughter.

She shut her eyes and shook her head, trying to shake it away.

But the laughter wouldn't stop.

She recognized it now. The low, throaty laughter she'd heard before—Chrissy's laughter when she floated in the moonlight.

"Stop!" Amanda cried aloud. "Please, stop!"

chapter

9

Wrong Number

*E*arly the next morning Amanda peered nervously down the hall. Chrissy's bedroom door was closed.

It's now or never, Amanda told herself. I'll have to move fast before anyone wakes up.

She hadn't slept more than an hour or two, but Amanda felt surprisingly awake. Every nerve was on alert. It was as if some kind of new energy coursed through her.

She silently made her way down to the kitchen, swinging the door closed. She picked up the red wall phone and punched in the numbers. The Shadyside area code first, then the number of Suzi Banton, her neighbor on Fear Street.

Luckily, Suzi had her own number, so Amanda wouldn't wake up the whole household.

Come on, Suzi, Amanda thought impatiently as the phone rang. I really need your help.

Four rings. Five. Finally Suzi's sleep-filled voice came on the line. "Hello?"

"Hi, Suzi. It's me, Amanda."

"Huh? Amanda? This had better be important. I was just having the most wonderful dream that I was out on a sailboat in the sunset with—"

"It *is* important," Amanda cut her off impatiently. "Super important."

"Why are you whispering?" Suzi demanded. "What's up?"

"I need a favor," Amanda said.

"I can't lend you any money," Suzi replied, yawning. "I couldn't find a job this summer, remember?"

"It's more important than money," Amanda whispered. "Could you go the Shadyside library for me? Look in the back newspapers. I need anything you can find on a family named Minor. Lilith Minor, Anton Minor, any Minor."

"Well . . ." Suzi hesitated. "Who are these people?"

"I don't have time to explain," said Amanda. "But this is a matter of life or death, Suzi. It's really really important to me."

"Do I have to?" Suzi moaned. "It sounds too much like schoolwork."

"Suzi—please! The Seahaven library is so tiny. I passed it on my way to school yesterday. It's like a doll library. I'm sure they won't have back issues of

59

newspapers," Amanda said. "Besides, you sort of owe me."

"What for?" Amanda's friend demanded.

"For all the times I've seen you climbing out of your bedroom window and down your maple tree to meet Pete Goodwin. I've never once told anyone."

"Oh, all right," Suzi agreed. "Like how many papers do you expect me to look through?"

"Start with the *Harrison County Gazette*," Amanda told her. "You don't have to go back farther than two years. Just do your best to find out anything you can."

"At least tell me what this is about?"

"I told you, I don't have time to explain now. It has to do with the mother's helper my parents hired. There's something weird about her."

"Who *isn't* weird?" Suzi replied dryly. "Oh, by the way," she added, sounding fully awake. "Speaking of mother's helpers, how's algebra?"

"Not bad. I met a cute guy."

"Oh, I get it now. Tell me if this is right. The nanny is after your new boyfriend. I'm right, right?"

"No way!" Amanda said sharply. "It's a lot more serious than that."

"What could be more serious than that?" Suzi said, laughing. "If that's it, I'll get right on the case. You can count on me, Amanda. No problem."

Upstairs, Amanda heard sounds of people moving around. A shower turned on. A toilet flushed. Time to get off the phone.

"Thanks a million, Suzi. I've got to go," Amanda said quickly. "Bye."

"Wait," Suzi insisted. "I almost forgot. Did that blond girl ever find you?"

"What blond girl?"

"The girl who came to your door right after your family left. I was walking by, and she asked about your family. She said she was a cousin or something. I told her that your family was vacationing in Seahaven."

"What did she look like?" Amanda asked.

"She was kind of pretty with—"

Amanda didn't hear the rest. She pulled the receiver from her ear.

"Hey!" The phone suddenly grew warm and soft in her hand. She stared at it in amazement. The receiver became so soft, her fingers were slipping into it.

And then the blood came pouring out.

Down Amanda's hand. Down her arm.

"Ohhhh." She let out a weak cry as she felt it trickle so warmly down her skin.

Not blood.

Not blood. But the red coloring of the phone receiver.

Trickling down her arm. So hot—so burning hot.

The mouthpiece took on an oozy, dripping shape. Strands of stringy red plastic stretched nearly down to the floor.

"Amanda? Amanda? What's going on?" She could hear Suzi's shouts through the melting, bleeding receiver.

"Suzi, what did she look like?" Amanda shouted frantically into the burning mouthpiece.

"She was beautiful," came Suzi's laughing reply.

Amanda froze in horror.

That isn't Suzi, she realized. It's not her voice. It's not Suzi. It's Chrissy!

But how could that be? This was the only phone in the house. There were no extensions.

"Better get to school, Amanda," Chrissy's husky voice burst through the pulsing phone.

The mouthpiece of the receiver fell onto the linoleum floor with a sickening *plop*. The red blob quivered as if it had taken on a life of its own.

Trembling, Amanda just stared down at it.

Chrissy's voice kept coming out of the red blob. "Why are you so curious about that girl, Amanda? Why are you so eager to know what she looked like? Don't worry your pretty little head. That girl will find you at the right time. And when she finds you—when she finds you, Amanda dear—you'll be sorry."

chapter

10

Blood Shed

*H*er heart racing, Amanda tore up the stairs and down the hall toward her parents' room.

"Mom! Dad!" she cried as she burst through their doorway. "The phone! You have to see the phone!"

When they saw it puddled in a red heap on the kitchen floor, they'd *have* to believe her!

"Huh?" Amanda cried out, astonished to find their room empty.

What was that metallic, clanking sound coming from outside?

She peered out their bedroom window, surprised to see a tow truck hooking up the family's mashed station wagon. Her parents stood watching in the driveway. She hadn't even heard them leave the house.

Amanda turned away from the window and spotted Chrissy's reference sheet lying on a night table. She snapped it up, folding it into the back pocket of her denim shorts.

Today I'll make Mom check Chrissy's references once and for all, she promised herself. But when they see the destroyed phone, that might not even be necessary. Chrissy will be gone.

Amanda hurried back downstairs to the kitchen. She stopped in the doorway—and gaped in surprise.

"Oh, no!"

The red phone sat in its cradle as if nothing had ever happened to it.

She stifled a scream of frustration. *What is going on here?*

An icy shiver ran down her entire body.

Am I losing it?

Am I totally losing it?

A flaming newspaper clipping? A melting phone?

If I tell my parents, they'll have me locked up for sure!

Amanda glanced around the kitchen. Where *was* Chrissy, anyway?

From their uncovered cage, Salt and Pepper warbled brightly.

Chrissy wasn't in the house. Amanda could tell that much from the happy songs of the birds.

And I'm not going to stick around until Chrissy shows up, Amanda decided.

She grabbed her canvas purse, hurried out back,

and pulled the bike from the shed. Chrissy had been right about one thing. She *was* going to be late for summer school if she didn't hurry.

The tow truck pulled away as Amanda came around to the front of the house. "How are you feeling?" her mother called as Amanda pedaled near.

"Fine," Amanda called back. *Never better.*

In town she stopped at a public phone near the Seahaven General Store. She called Suzi again. Mrs. Banton answered. "Suzi said she was going to the library or something," Mrs. Banton told Amanda, sounding puzzled.

"Thanks. Bye." Good old Suzi—grumpy but reliable. Amanda prayed Suzi would find something useful.

Continuing on to Seahaven High, Amanda parked her bike and jogged to Room Ten. Dave Malone smiled when she walked in. Amanda smiled back.

She took the closest seat to Dave she could find. How ironic, she thought, that she loved being in algebra class.

Everything is so *normal* here, she thought as she opened her algebra book. The thing I dreaded most—summer school—is turning out to be my one bright spot of sanity.

"Get together with your partner," Mrs. Taylor told them toward the end of class.

Dave slid over beside Amanda. "We're in luck," he said. "We're still in the chapter I understand."

"Great," Amanda said, smiling at him.

"Yeah, enjoy it while you can. Next week we start cosines and that stuff. That makes no sense to me at all."

"I guess we'll have to struggle through together," Amanda said.

"I don't know," Dave said, shaking his head. "You may lose all respect for me when you see how bad I really am at this."

"You can't be worse than I am," Amanda assured him.

"This could get ugly," Dave whispered.

When class ended, Dave asked, "How's the mother's helper working out, the one you were curious about the other day?"

Amanda shook her head grimly. "Don't ask. You'd never believe it."

"Try me," he said softly.

Amanda gathered her books. Dave walked with her toward the front of school. As they walked, she told him everything that had happened with Chrissy. "You think I'm insane, right?" Amanda said as they reached the front lawn.

"You don't seem nuts to me," Dave said seriously. "There's no reason for you to make these things up."

His words encircled Amanda like a warm hug. It was wonderful to be believed. "I'm not crazy. Really. All these things happened. I don't know why or how. But they did."

"You've got to get her out of the house," Dave urged in a low voice.

"How? How do I do that?" Amanda asked hopelessly.

"Well—we'll have to think about it." He brushed a hand back through his wavy hair. "I asked around about her. Nobody I talked to ever heard of a Lorraine, Eloise, or Chrissy Minor."

Amanda pulled Chrissy's résumé from her shorts pocket. "She says she lives at Three Old Sea Road."

"Unless her aunt is a ghost, she doesn't live there," Dave replied, staring at the résumé. "That old house has been empty for years. They say a bunch of people were murdered in there. Weird story. The caretaker's son is a friend of mine. Come on," he said. "You need a break. Do you have some time?"

"Sure," Amanda replied, taking his hand.

Dave put Amanda's bike in the backseat of his blue '78 Mustang. They drove off, heading out of town.

Slowly they climbed the steep road that ran along the shore, rising high above it. Amanda pointed out the road where she would have turned off to go back to her summerhouse.

As he drove, Dave motioned to a wide gate. "There's a huge house down that drive that has been boarded up for a few years now," he said.

"Wow, it's as creepy as Fear Street around here," Amanda commented.

"Fear Street?" His expression became confused.

"It's a very long story," Amanda replied with a sigh.

They drove on to the top of the hill. Dave pulled into a crescent-shaped parking lot. It was empty except for a phone booth. "This is Channings Bluff. It's an official scenic overlook," Dave told her. "Want to check it out?"

"Sure," Amanda agreed with a smile. She climbed out of the car and made her way to the split-rail fence. Shading her eyes against the sun, she gazed out past it.

A steep rocky drop stretched below. Three large boulders jutted out from the side of the bluff. Beneath them the ocean churned. Several boulders poked up from the ocean floor.

"See those three boulders sticking out of the side?" Dave asked. "My older brother and his friends painted really messed-up pictures of our principal, vice principal, and dean on them about four years ago. We call it Seahaven's own Mount Rushmore."

"I can't see the faces," said Amanda, leaning over the fence, shielding her eyes with one hand.

"No. But boats out on the ocean can see them," Dave said, snickering. "My brother is so weird!"

"How did they get down there?" Amanda asked.

"They tied the paint and brushes to their belts, then they tied ropes to these fences and lowered themselves. It was totally insane."

A few minutes later Amanda and Dave left

68

Channings Bluff and drove down the road to the Beachside Inn. They parked in front.

"Do you have a bathing suit?" Dave asked as they got out of the car.

"Yeah," Amanda replied. "I have one on under my clothes."

Dave led the way to the beach behind the inn. "My brother Mike works here," he explained, pointing to the rental shed.

"Is he the rock painter?" Amanda asked.

"No. That's my other brother, Ed."

At the shed, Dave greeted a guy with curly red hair who stood behind the rental counter. "Mike, how about letting us have a wave-runner for a while."

"I guess so," Mike agreed. "No one has rented one all week. I don't think there'll be a sudden rush of wave-runner rentals today."

"Not likely," Dave agreed. "How about that blue one over there? The two-seater."

"Okay, take it."

Amanda followed Dave over to one of three wave-runners lined up at the shoreline next to the sailboats. "Just keep your arms around me," Dave instructed as Amanda climbed onto the seat behind him.

"Okay," Amanda agreed. She realized she felt a little shy about leaning up so close to him and wrapping her arms around his waist.

"Hold on now!" Dave called back to her.

Amanda tightened her grip around him. She

liked his warm, soapy smell. She felt safe and happy holding on to him.

A few moments later they were out on the ocean, moving fast. The fine ocean spray tickled Amanda's cheeks. Her hair whipped around her face. It felt as if they were riding a motorcycle over the top of the choppy water.

Before long, a small patch of land came into sight. Dave headed right for it. He slowed down and stopped the wave-runner on the rocky shore of the small island. "I want to show you my secret hideout," he said, taking her hand.

She followed him through foliage and trees. Finally they came to a broken-down woodshed. "There it is!" Dave exclaimed, gesturing proudly toward the shed.

"This is the secret hideout?" Amanda asked.

"Wait until you see the inside," Dave replied.

Amanda followed him in. "Wow!" she cried out, startled. The shed was furnished with a chair, a cot, and a table. Amanda spotted blankets, two trunks, lanterns, flashlights, and shovels. "What is all this?" she asked.

"Mike and I found this shed three years ago," Dave explained. "It was used by hunters. They'd hunt geese and ducks and even raccoons. But hunting is illegal around here, and the game wardens were always on their cases. At first the hunters just hid their stuff out here, but when the warden threatened to have them arrested, they finally gave up. I guess they were afraid to even come back for their stuff."

"There's a *lot* of stuff here," Amanda noted.

"Yeah, a lot of neat stuff," Dave agreed. "Mike and I call this place the blood shed."

Amanda wrinkled her nose in distaste. "I don't get it. Why *blood* shed?"

"Look down," Dave told her.

"Oh!" Amanda leaped back. The floorboards under her feet were stained a deep brownish red. "Do you think that's really blood?"

"Yeah," Dave nodded solemnly.

"Animal blood, right?" Amanda said, remembering this was a hunters' shed.

"Probably," Dave agreed. "And that blood just gave me a great idea. I know exactly how you can get rid of Chrissy."

His eyes lit up. He began digging excitedly through the trunk he'd opened.

Amanda shuddered in fright as Dave pulled a long, gleaming knife from the trunk. He held it above his head triumphantly. "Here it is!" His eyes danced wildly. "You can use this."

Huh? Is he *crazy?* Amanda wondered, taking a step back.

Dave followed her, looming close, his eyes wide with excitement. He brandished the long knife in front of Amanda's face.

"If you don't want to," he said, lowering his voice, "I'll do it."

11

A Knife Trick

Amanda gasped. "You're kidding—right?"

He shook his head, an odd smile forming on his excited face.

"But, Dave, I can't *kill* her!" Amanda protested shrilly.

"No, not kill her," Dave replied breathlessly. "That's dumb. My plan is better than that."

"What plan?" Amanda demanded, staring at the gleaming knife blade.

"Plant it in her room. You know, in a dresser drawer or something. Then make sure your parents find it. When they see that Chrissy is hiding a knife like this, they'll bounce her out of there in a second!"

Amanda let her breath out in a relieved *whoosh*.

Dave handed Amanda the knife.

She took it reluctantly. She felt a cold chill on the back of her neck as she spotted seven notches cut into the ivory handle. "Do you think these notches show how many animals were skinned with this knife?"

"Could be," Dave replied. "They probably skinned them right in here. That explains the blood all over the place."

"For a minute there I thought you were totally nuts!" Amanda confessed.

"That's all right," he replied, grinning. "My brothers and I have done some nutty stuff. But I don't think we're actively insane."

They both laughed.

"But I really think my idea about Chrissy might work," he insisted.

Amanda glanced at the knife in her hand. "It's a little—I don't know. It's a little out there—you know, extreme. Don't you think?"

"I think Chrissy sounds a little out there," Dave replied. "And I think you should do whatever it takes to get rid of her."

He ripped open a white box and pulled out a cellophane bag. "Want some dried apple?" he offered, holding open the bag. "This place is completely stocked with dried foods. Dehydrated hamburgers, powdered milk, everything. Mike and I used to make up these weird adventure fantasies. You know. Like aliens had invaded the planet and we had to hide out here."

73

Dave grinned at her. "I shouldn't be telling you all my weird secrets. Just a minute ago you thought I was nuts."

"Those kinds of fantasies are fun. I don't think that's nuts," Amanda assured him.

"Good," Dave replied. "Mike and I spent hours making up wild stories about this shed. It sounds crazy, but I guess you never know what could happen."

"That's for sure," said Amanda, her thoughts returning to Chrissy.

"Don't worry," Dave told her. "It'll work out all right."

Amanda gazed up into his soft, sympathetic eyes. The next thing she knew, they were kissing. Slowly. Tenderly.

Dave stroked her hair. "Don't worry. You're not in this alone," he whispered. "I'll help you."

"Like with algebra?" Amanda asked.

"Yeah, like that," he replied, smiling. "Neither of us knows what's going on, but we'll get through it."

Amanda smiled. For the first time in days the cold hand of fear released its grip a little. At last she had a friend.

"I'd better get back," Amanda said. "My parents will be wondering where I am."

"Are you going to take the knife?" Dave asked.

Amanda stared at it lying on the low wooden table.

Would Dave's plan work?

Would the knife be enough to get Chrissy out of the house for good?

Impulsively, she grabbed it.

"Okay," she said, staring hard at the gleaming, long blade. "Okay. I'll do it."

Amanda felt carefree as they drove home. Riding in the car with Dave was like being in a safe, happy place. They laughed and sang along with the radio all the way back.

But as the car pulled up the driveway, Amanda's good mood disappeared. Home again, she thought glumly. Home with Chrissy and the family who adores her. My family.

Dave took Amanda's hand as they walked to the front door. Amanda pushed open the door. Chrissy stood in the living room, looking fantastic in white short shorts and a heather-gray midriff top.

"Hi," Chrissy greeted them pleasantly. Amanda didn't like the way Chrissy's blue eyes widened appreciatively at the sight of Dave.

Chrissy tossed her silky hair over her shoulder. "Amanda, you didn't tell me you had such a good-looking friend," she said.

"He's from Seahaven," Amanda said pointedly. "I thought all you Seahaven people knew one another."

"I'm not from Seahaven," Chrissy said flatly.

"Your address is Three Old Sea Road," Amanda insisted.

"Oh, Aunt Lorraine is buying that old house. But we're not moved into it yet. I put that on my résumé because I thought we'd be in it by now. But you know how those things go."

"Where do you live?" Dave asked pleasantly.

"My aunt and I live in Seaport," Chrissy told him.

"That's the town next to Seahaven," Dave told Amanda.

"Are you sure you don't mean Harrison County?" Amanda asked, referring to the clipping from the *Harrison County Gazette*.

The flirtatious smile Chrissy aimed at Dave didn't slip for a moment.

Amanda felt disappointed to see Chrissy so unruffled by the reference to Harrison County.

"No, not Harrison County," said Chrissy. "Seaport." She turned her attention to Dave. "I heard a car pull up. What do you drive?"

"A seventy-eight Mustang," Dave told her.

"That's a classic!" Chrissy exclaimed, moving closer to Dave. "Would you show it to me?"

With a darting glance at her bag, Dave reminded Amanda of the knife.

Amanda realized he was right. If he could get Chrissy outside, she could go plant the knife.

"Are you interested in old cars?" Dave asked Chrissy.

"Totally," Chrissy replied.

"Come on. I'll show it to you."

Amanda glared at the back of Chrissy's head as she followed Dave out the door.

The moment the door shut behind them, she hurried up to Chrissy's room. Not wasting a moment, she darted across the room and pulled open the top dresser drawer. Chrissy's silky white underthings were neatly folded inside.

With a trembling hand, Amanda took the knife from her bag. The blade shimmered in the sunlight.

Amanda felt cold all over. She realized she hated holding it.

Without warning something strange happened to the knife. A bead of red slowly formed on its tip.

Amanda studied it curiously.

What's happening? she wondered.

She brought the knife up close, trying to see what was causing the stain.

Then, as she gaped in startled horror, a bright red spray shot out of the knife blade.

Blood! Amanda realized.

It's spraying *blood!* All over me!

chapter

12

Ruffled Feathers

With a terrified cry, Amanda hurled the knife at the dresser.

Spewing bright red blood, it hit the dresser top and tumbled into the open drawer.

Amanda stared helplessly, frozen by her shock, watching as Chrissy's things were drenched in red.

"This isn't happening!" she cried out loud, her voice tiny and choked.

"This *can't* be happening!"

Before she realized it, she was running. Down the stairs to the living room. The empty living room.

Where were her parents? Why weren't they there to help her?

"Ohhhh." A low gasp of horror escaped Amanda's throat as she saw the birdcage.

She took a step closer. One more. Then stopped.

"Noooo!"

Her frantic wail revealed her shock.

Salt and Pepper lay dead in their cages.

"Their throats—" Amanda murmured, wrapping a cold hand around her own throat. "Their throats are *cut!*"

In answer to Amanda's shrieks, Mrs. Conklin came racing in from the deck. "Amanda—what on earth?" she cried breathlessly. "You're covered in blood. You're—"

Amanda pointed, one hand still around her throat, as if protecting it.

Her mother gasped. "Oh, no—"

Neither of them moved. A heavy silence fell over the room.

Dimly Amanda became aware of the front door opening and closing. Someone had come into the house and hurried upstairs. But Amanda couldn't even wonder who it was. She felt numb all over, too terrified to feel anything.

Mrs. Conklin spoke first. "Amanda, I don't understand this. How could you?"

Amanda stared blankly at her mother. What was she talking about?

Chrissy burst into the room. She held the bloody knife high in her hand. The blade was stained with red blood.

"Mrs. Conklin!" Chrissy cried breathlessly. "I found this in my top drawer. There's blood all over everything! All my stuff is ruined! All ruined!"

She stopped short at the sight of Amanda's

blood-drenched clothing. Her eyes traveled over to the dead birds.

"Oh, no!" Chrissy cried, raising her hands to the sides of her face. "The birds! They're—they're—" She narrowed her eyes at Amanda. "The blood in my drawer—it's from them?"

"Don't act innocent!" Amanda shrieked, balling her hands into tight fists. "Don't pretend, Chrissy! You did this! You! I don't know how—but it was you!"

Chrissy gasped and covered her mouth with one hand. Her eyes widened in confusion. "How can you say that, Amanda? How can you say such horrible things about me? Why do you *hate* me so much?"

Once again Amanda felt herself slip out of control. But she couldn't stop herself. "You're evil!" she screamed at Chrissy. "You're evil and I want you out of my house! I want you out *now!*"

Amanda's father burst into the room. "Calm down, Amanda!" he cried angrily. "Take a deep breath! Don't say another word!"

He turned to Mrs. Conklin. "Has she tried to hurt Chrissy again?"

"No!" Amanda wailed desperately. "No—please! No! Don't turn against me! Be on my side! Please! Be on my side!"

Amanda stared at them. These were her parents. They *had* to be on her side.

Didn't they?

"The birds have been killed," Mrs. Conklin told her husband softly. "Chrissy found the knife in her dresser drawer."

"I can't take any more of this," Mr. Conklin said, sighing. "We have to find a doctor for Amanda—right now."

chapter

13

Bad News

The next morning Amanda sat in the office of Dr. Elmont, a psychiatrist. Amanda guessed he was about sixty. He had gray hair and dark, penetrating eyes.

He didn't say much. He sat back in his large brown leather chair and folded his arms, nodding as Amanda spoke.

Amanda had been reluctant to talk at first. But once she got started, it felt good to unload the whole story. Slowly, trying to remain calm, she told him everything that happened since Chrissy had arrived.

When she finished, she waited for the doctor to reply.

"You've been through a lot," he said finally,

shifting back in his chair, stretching his arms above his head.

"Then you believe me?" Amanda asked, feeling her spirits lift.

"I believe that you believe what you are saying," he said.

Amanda felt as if he had just slugged her in the chest.

He didn't think she was a liar. He just thought she was nuts.

"Do you feel that when you failed algebra, you let your parents down?" he asked.

Tears pooled in Amanda's dark eyes. "This isn't about algebra. Not at all," she insisted.

"Let me suggest something and see how it hits you," said Dr. Elmont. "Maybe somewhere deep inside, you think you don't deserve your parents' love anymore since you failed algebra. Maybe you think Chrissy is taking your place, and you hate her for that."

One tear slid down Amanda's cheek as she let her head drop in despair. "You've got it all wrong," she murmured. "That's not true."

Dr. Elmont walked around his desk. He came up to Amanda and patted her shoulder. "Don't cry. This will all work itself out. Let me talk to your parents in private a moment."

Wiping the tears off her cheeks, Amanda made her way into the waiting room. Her parents glanced up from their chairs. They both looked pale and solemn. "Dr. Elmont wants to see you," Amanda mumbled.

"You don't look like you feel any better," her mother observed.

"I don't," Amanda answered curtly.

Dr. Elmont appeared at the door. "We'll be right back, honey," said Mrs. Conklin.

Amanda sat and waited, wondering what Dr. Elmont was saying to them. Was he telling them to lock her up in an institution?

She sighed and shook her head, trying to force back the tears.

Time dragged on. Her parents seemed to be in there forever.

When they finally emerged from the inner office, their expressions were grim. Dr. Elmont stepped out behind them.

"So, Amanda, you are going to see me again in five days," he told her. "If you need to speak to me before then, call. Take one of my cards from the receptionist's desk. Above all, try to relax on the beach and put all this out of your head."

Amanda nodded numbly as she took a card from the front desk. She hoped her parents hadn't paid a lot of money for that advice. *Relax and forget it.* Thanks loads, Doc!

"What did he have to say about me?" Amanda asked as they walked across the small parking lot to the car they'd rented while the station wagon was being repaired.

"He thinks that failing algebra put you under a

lot of stress," said her father. "He thinks that failure brought up fears of rejection, and that subconsciously you're afraid we want to replace you with Chrissy."

"That's what he said to me. But it's not true," Amanda told them.

"This is all going on below the level of your conscious mind, Amanda," said Mrs. Conklin. "You can't control it. That's why Dr. Elmont wants you to relax, to lessen the stress you feel."

Amanda climbed into the backseat of the car and lay down. The night before she hadn't been able to sleep. She shut her eyes. I could always sleep in the car when I was a kid, she thought. Maybe I can sleep now.

A few minutes later Amanda heard her mother whisper, "Amanda, are you awake?"

Amanda didn't feel like answering. She really wanted to be left alone. She decided to let them think she was asleep.

"She's out," Mrs. Conklin whispered to her husband. "John, don't you think we should fire Chrissy?"

"We can't now," Mr. Conklin said quietly. "You heard what Dr. Elmont said."

"I know," said Mrs. Conklin with a sigh. "If we fire Chrissy, we'll be supporting Amanda's false fears about her. And we don't want to do that, do we? We don't want to give Amanda the message that she is right. That Chrissy is a threat to her."

"What he said makes sense," whispered Mr.

Conklin. "If she thinks Chrissy is really a threat, then eventually someone else will come along whom she feels threatened by. And she'll start this crazy behavior all over again."

"I know, I know," Mrs. Conklin said with an air of sad resignation. "It's better to let Chrissy stay and have Amanda work through her feelings right now."

"So Chrissy stays," Mr. Conklin confirmed.

Amanda's heart pounded as she listened from the backseat.

Chrissy is evil! she wanted to shout.

Why are you falling for all of Dr. Elmont's mumbo jumbo?

Chrissy is evil! There's nothing more to be said!

Amanda thought hard all the way home.

What can I do? What can I do now?

By the time they pulled up the gravel driveway, Amanda had an idea. She would let everyone think she accepted Dr. Elmont's theory. It would get her parents off her back. And it would put Chrissy off guard.

Pretending that she had been deeply asleep, Amanda yawned and stretched as she followed her parents into the house. They found Chrissy playing Monopoly on the floor with Kyle, while Merry watched "Sesame Street" on the TV.

Chrissy looked lovely in a white cotton sundress, her hair pulled back with a pink satin ribbon. Amanda noticed with amusement that Chrissy seemed to wear white a lot.

Because she's so pure, Amanda thought. Pure evil.

"How did it go?" Chrissy asked sweetly.

"Pretty good," Amanda replied. "Can I talk to you out on the deck, Chrissy?"

"Sure," Chrissy agreed. "Excuse me, Kyle."

"No problem," said Kyle. He gazed up at Amanda sadly. Poor Kyle, Amanda thought. He obviously thinks his sister has become a nut case.

Out on the deck, an ocean breeze blew softly. It was a perfect summer day. "Listen, Chrissy," Amanda started. "Dr. Elmont says this is all—you know—all in my head. He says I'm insecure about you or something. So, I want to apologize. Really. I'm sorry about the way I've been acting. Sorry about—everything."

Amanda let out a long breath. There. That was a first step in making things better—or pretending to, at least.

"I understand," Chrissy replied solemnly. "I hope we can be friends."

Just then, Amanda felt something soft brush against her ankle. "A kitten!" she cried out delightedly.

A tiny calico had wandered up onto the deck. Amanda knelt and picked her up. "Where did you come from, little lady?" she said, recalling that all cats with calico markings are female.

The kitten's purr was like a small motor running inside it. Abruptly, the purring stopped. The kitten bared her tiny fangs and hissed at Chrissy.

"You'd better put that thing down," Chrissy warned tensely. "It might be diseased. You shouldn't touch stray animals. Look how crazy it's acting."

Alarms went off in Amanda's head as she thought of Mr. Jinx. She stared sharply at Chrissy.

Why did animals hate her?

Amanda set the kitten down on the deck and watched it run away.

"Good. Let him go back to wherever he came from," said Chrissy. Her expression brightened. "Do you want to come in and play Monopoly with us?"

"No thanks," Amanda replied. "Maybe I'll just take a walk down to the beach."

"All right. I'm glad we're making a fresh start, Amanda."

"Me too," Amanda agreed.

Chrissy disappeared inside, and Amanda headed down toward the pool. As she reached the shed, she heard the kitten meowing. She saw it in the shadow of the shed wall, as if it were hiding.

"What's wrong, girl?" Amanda asked, stooping down. "Are you lost? Did somebody dump you off in the woods?"

In reply, the kitten nuzzled Amanda's hand.

"Come on," Amanda said quietly as she scooped up the kitten. "I'll sneak you into my room. I don't want to upset Chrissy now that she and I are supposed to be friends."

Amanda carried the cat over to the pool. Wrapping the tiny thing in a beach towel, she carried her around to the front of the house.

Chrissy and Kyle were concentrating on their Monopoly game. It was easy for Amanda to sneak the cat up to her room. Then she crept down to the pantry and pulled out an unopened bag of dried cat food that had been bought for Mr. Jinx.

Back in her room, Amanda mashed the dried food with a pencil and set it out on a fashion magazine for the kitten to eat. While she watched her gobble down the food, Amanda stretched out on the bed.

A knock on the door stirred Amanda.

She sat up, confused.

Gray light filtered in through the window.

She realized she must have slept for most of the day.

"Amanda, are you awake? Phone for you," came her mother's voice through the door.

Suzi! Amanda guessed. "Stay here and be quiet," she whispered to the kitten as she slipped out the door.

The kitchen phone receiver had been set on the counter for her. Amanda picked it up eagerly. "Hi. Suzi?"

"This isn't Suzi," a familiar female voice said. "It's me."

"Carter?" Amanda cried, surprised. Carter Phillips was a friend of Suzi's. Amanda knew Carter from Shadyside High, but they had never really been friends. "What's up?"

"Did you hear about Suzi?" Carter began, sounding strained.

"No. Hear what?" Amanda asked.

"No, of course not. How *could* you know?" Carter replied. Then her voice broke, and she uttered a sob. "It—it's bad, Amanda. It's real bad."

"Huh?" Amanda gasped. "What's bad, Carter? What do you mean?"

chapter

14

Get Out Now!

"**S**uzi is in the hospital," Carter said in a trembling voice.

"What?" Amanda wasn't sure she heard correctly. "What happened?"

"She was in the library yesterday, looking up something," Carter continued. "It—it's so *weird*, Amanda. Suddenly she slumped over on the microfilm viewer, blood pouring from her mouth and nose."

"How horrible!" Amanda cried, clutching the phone tightly. "What was it?"

"The doctors are totally puzzled," Carter said. "They haven't a clue. They're keeping Suzi in the hospital for tests."

Amanda felt a knot of dread in her stomach. Chrissy had done this! She was absolutely sure of it.

Chrissy had been on the phone line the day before when Amanda had talked to Suzi. Somehow Chrissy had used her powers on Suzi.

"Amanda, are you there?" Carter asked.

"Uh—yeah. I'm sorry. I was thinking about something. This is so terrible!"

"I know. Today I went to get the things Suzi had left behind at the library. Mrs. Banton asked me to. The librarian told me Suzi was checking on microfilmed back issues of the *Harrison County Gazette* when—when it happened. Mrs. Banton has no idea why she was doing it. Suzi isn't exactly the type to do research when she doesn't have to."

"How did you know to call me?" Amanda asked, still thinking about Chrissy.

"Suzi had your summer phone number written on a notebook, so I thought I'd call to see if you could tell me anything that might help. She wasn't taking any weird drugs or anything, was she?"

"Huh? Suzi? Of course not!" Amanda replied in a quavering voice. She realized that her hand was shaking so violently that she couldn't even hold the phone to her ear properly.

"Do you know why she was checking those old newspapers?" Carter asked.

"No, no idea." How could she possibly explain to Carter everything that had been happening? "Carter, I have to go. Call me tomorrow and let me know how Suzi is, okay?"

"All right," Carter agreed. "She can't have any visitors, but I'll call Mrs. Banton and check."

"Thanks," Amanda said as she hung up. She stared at the phone, trying to stop shaking, thinking hard.

Now I know one thing for sure, she decided. I have to get into Chrissy's room and see the rest of those clippings. They have the answer to Chrissy's real identity and purpose.

Mrs. Conklin came into the kitchen. "Amanda, you're pale as a ghost. What's wrong?"

"Suzi Banton's in the hospital," she told her mother.

Mrs. Conklin's face filled with surprise. "What happened?"

"I'm not sure. The doctors aren't sure either." That was all she was going to say. If she told her mother what she suspected about Chrissy, her parents would rush her back to Dr. Elmont first thing in the morning.

"How did your talk with Chrissy go?" Mrs. Conklin asked.

Amanda's eyes shifted restlessly for a moment. What should she say about Chrissy? She stuck to her decision to act as if she had really made peace with Chrissy. "It went great, Mom. What Dr. Elmont said really made sense to me. I'm going to get along with Chrissy from now on."

Mrs. Conklin studied Amanda. "I hope so, honey."

"Yeah, don't worry, Mom."

"Okay, if you say so. Listen, the Bakers called

and invited your dad and me. It's Chrissy's night off. Do you feel well enough to mind the kids?"

Amanda turned to see Chrissy appear in the doorway. "I'll stay if you need me," she offered.

"No, that's okay. You can go out, Chrissy," Amanda told her, flashing her a warm smile.

If Chrissy went out, Amanda realized, it would be the perfect chance to search the clippings and phone the references on Chrissy's résumé. "Really. The kids are all ready for bed anyway. There's not much to do."

"I don't have anything planned," Chrissy replied. "You've had a hard time, and I don't mind staying."

"You girls can work this out yourselves." Mrs. Conklin laughed. "As long as one of you stays, we're going."

"I'll stay," Amanda said firmly.

"Then at least let me go tuck the kids in and say good night," said Chrissy. "They get upset if I don't do that."

Chrissy hurried off to tuck them in. Mrs. Conklin kissed Amanda on the forehead. "I guess you two really are going to be friends. I'm so glad. Thanks for staying."

"No problem."

A few minutes later Mr. and Mrs. Conklin drove away. Amanda returned to her bedroom. She passed the room Kyle and Merry were sharing. Chrissy sat on the bed reading *The Cat in the Hat Comes Back* to Merry.

In her bedroom Amanda found the copy of Chrissy's résumé. "You stay in here," she warned the calico kitten. "If you want to stay alive, I've got to hide you from Chrissy."

Amanda hurried back to the kitchen. As she passed, she heard Chrissy reading another book to Merry. Closing the door behind her, Amanda crossed the room to the kitchen phone. She punched in the second number listed, the one which no one had ever answered before.

One ring. Two. Three. Four. Amanda gave up on the seventh ring.

So much for that, thought Amanda. She glanced at the kitchen door, then punched in the first number, the one which was always busy.

This time someone picked up right away. "Hello?"

"Oh, hello," said Amanda, startled that someone had answered. "I'm calling about Chrissy Minor. She gave this number as a reference." Amanda checked the name above the number. Elaine Harriman. "She said to speak to Mrs. Harriman."

"Well—" The girl on the other end hesitated. "I'm just a neighbor. My mother and I—we came into the judge's house. We were wondering why we hadn't seen the Harrimans in so long. You won't believe what we just found. I—I'm sorry. I think I'm going to be sick. It's so—"

At that moment Amanda heard a woman call, "Who's on the phone, Rachel?"

"It's someone calling about Chrissy."

95

"Hang up right now," Amanda heard the older woman command.

"No—please!" Amanda begged. "Don't hang up."

"I can't talk now," the girl said, lowering her voice. "Did you say this is about a reference? Do you know where Chrissy is?"

"Yes, she's right here."

"Chrissy is in your house!?" the girl gasped in horror. "Oh, no! Get out—now!"

"Why?" asked Amanda. "Why?"

The phone went dead.

chapter

15

A Picture of Surprise

Amanda stared at the silent phone in shock.

She glanced up to see Chrissy standing in the doorway, her arms folded across her white dress. "Is something wrong with the phone?" Chrissy asked, a strange smile on her face.

"No, it's fine," Amanda replied, hanging up quickly. "I was just trying to remember someone's phone number."

"Suzi Banton's number?" Chrissy asked.

Amanda's heart fluttered. "No." Was Chrissy about to admit what she had done to Suzi?

Chrissy crossed to the refrigerator. "Your mother told me about your friend Suzi. What a shame."

Amanda waited for more. But Chrissy just stepped to the cabinet and took out a glass.

Amanda hurried down the hall, her mind racing. That girl on the phone had said to get out. What had she found in the Harriman house? Whatever it was, she said it was sickening.

What had Chrissy done?

Horrifying pictures crowded Amanda's mind. She had to push them out. If she let her imagination run wild, she knew she'd totally panic.

She slowed her pace when she got to the room Kyle and Merry shared. "Everything okay in there?" she called into the room.

"Yeah, but Chrissy said she was going to bring me a glass of milk. Where is she?" Kyle called from his bed, where he flipped through a comic book. Merry slept peacefully.

"Okay. Coming right up," Amanda said, turning back.

Should she listen to that girl on the phone?

Should she get the kids out of the house?

Where would they go?

Besides, her parents would bring them right back. Her parents would just think that Amanda had gone psycho again.

No, Amanda decided. It would be better to get Chrissy out tonight. Then she could look for the clippings, show her parents whatever she found, and hope it was enough to make them see for themselves that Chrissy was evil.

Amanda stopped at the kitchen door. It had been pulled shut.

Why?

She pulled it open a tiny bit and peeked in.

Chrissy had a small packet in her hand. She was pouring some kind of brownish powder into the milk.

Her heart pounding, Amanda leaned hard against the wall. What did that packet contain?

Poison?

I can't let Kyle drink that milk, she decided.

Taking a deep breath, Amanda pushed open the kitchen door. She leaned against the counter and tried to sound casual. "So, what have you decided to do on your big night off?"

"I told you—no plans," Chrissy replied. "Maybe I'll just stay in my room and write letters."

"That doesn't sound like fun," Amanda said, trying not to sound desperate. "Why don't you go to a movie? That new scary beach movie, *Blood Surfer,* is playing in town. I hear it's so bad, it's good."

"No thanks," Chrissy replied with a smile. "I hate scary movies." She picked up the milk.

Amanda wrapped her hand around the glass. "Let me take it to Kyle," she offered. "After all, it is your night off."

"Well, I guess so," Chrissy agreed. "Sure."

Sure, Amanda echoed darkly. You'd just love me to get blamed for killing my own brother, wouldn't you? After all, everyone thinks I'm totally nuts now, anyway—thanks to you, Chrissy.

"I'll just clean up a little in here," Chrissy said pleasantly.

Amanda left with the milk, wondering what to do with it. If she didn't give it to Kyle, he'd start screaming that he didn't get his milk. Then Chrissy would just whip him up another poison milk shake.

Amanda decided to stall until Chrissy went to her room or went out. Then she'd dump the milk.

As she stood thinking, the doorbell rang. Still holding the milk, she answered the door. It was Dave.

"Hi," he said, smiling. "You weren't in class today. So I brought over the assignments. Were you sick or something?"

Quickly and quietly she drew him inside. "No, I'm not sick. But I'm glad you're here," she whispered. "I'm pretty sure Chrissy has poisoned this milk. She wants me to take it to Kyle and—"

"Whoa!" he stopped her. "She *poisoned* this milk? What happened with the knife?"

Amanda squeezed his arm. "You won't believe it. It was the most horrible thing. I—"

Dave's hand swept past her, knocking the glass from her hands. It shattered loudly on the wood floor. "Oh, man! What a klutz!" he cried.

His darting glance caused Amanda to turn. Chrissy had just come out of the kitchen. It took Chrissy a moment to see what had happened. "No problem," she said quickly. "I'll just get a towel for that."

"Thanks," Amanda whispered as Chrissy disappeared into the kitchen. "That was fast thinking. I'll tell you about the knife later. Do you think you can distract her while I check out something in her room? Show her your car again or something? The more time you can give me, the—"

"Here we go," Chrissy sang out, returning. She stooped and mopped up the milk with a cloth. "No harm done," she said, gazing up at Dave with wide eyes. "Now I'd better get Kyle more milk. The only problem is, I think I used the last packet of chocolate. Do you think Kyle will drink it plain?"

"Huh?" Amanda gasped. "Chocolate?" The packet contained only chocolate? Am I getting totally paranoid? Amanda asked herself. Am I totally losing it?

She saw Dave staring at her, his expression questioning.

"Uh—I'll get the milk," Amanda volunteered eagerly.

"So, Dave, how's it going? I love your tan!" Chrissy said as Amanda made her way into the kitchen.

Very subtle, Chrissy! Why don't you just throw yourself at him? Amanda thought angrily as she opened the refrigerator.

"Blood Surfer is playing in town," she heard Dave say. "I asked Amanda to go, but she says she has to catch up on algebra. You wouldn't want to come, would you?"

"That'd be great," Chrissy replied. "I love scary movies, and I hear this one's so bad, it's good. Tonight's my night off too. Do you think Amanda will mind?"

"No, why should she? I'll tell her we're going," Dave said.

I guess Dave's taking Chrissy to the movies is the price I have to pay to get her out of the house, Amanda told herself as she poured the milk. It would be pretty dumb to get jealous.

"I'll go get my sweater up in my room," she heard Chrissy say.

Amanda hurried out of the kitchen. "Did you have to make a *date* with her?" she whispered.

"This will give you at least two hours," Dave whispered back.

"Just be careful around her," Amanda warned.

"Yeah, sure," Dave teased. "I won't let her give me any chocolate milk!"

Chrissy appeared on the stairs. "Did Dave tell you, Amanda? We're going to go see that movie you recommended. It's okay, isn't it?"

"Have a good time," Amanda replied flatly.

As soon as she heard Dave's car pull away, Amanda hurried up the stairs. "Here's your milk," she told Kyle, stepping into the kids' room. "Oh, he's asleep."

She took the book from Kyle's hand. Then she pulled Merry's blanket over her and turned off their light.

Back in the kitchen, she called the number of the

girl who had hung up on her. Maybe she'll be more willing to talk now, Amanda hoped.

But the phone rang and rang. No one picked up. The girl must have gone next door.

Sighing, Amanda hung up. "Now let's find those clippings," she murmured out loud.

Feeling her heart start to race, Amanda hurried up to Chrissy's room. The blue carpet still contained dark blood stains.

When she opened the top dresser drawer, Amanda was relieved to see that Chrissy's bloody things had been removed. Still, maroon splotches stained the inside of the drawer. Amanda shuddered at the memory.

No news clippings here, Amanda thought, closing the top drawer. She searched the dresser carefully, one drawer at a time.

Only clothing.

No sign of the newspaper stories.

Amanda opened the narrow closet. Standing on tiptoe, she pulled down a stack of shoe boxes from the top shelf. She opened each box and found— shoes.

The last box contained a pair of leather boots. Amanda couldn't resist taking a look at them. Lifting one from the tissue paper in the box, she turned the boot over in her hand. At least Chrissy has good taste, she thought.

As she returned the boot to the box, Amanda saw a corner of faded newspaper peeking out from beneath the tissue lining.

Excitedly Amanda lifted the tissue paper. "Yes!" she murmured softly. "I've found them!"

Amanda lifted the first clipping. She covered her mouth in complete surprise when she saw the photo next to the article.

It was a photo of her own father!

chapter

16

Lilith

Struggling to hold her hand steady, Amanda read quickly through the newspaper article:

Public Defender John Conklin of Shadyside will defend Arthur Lawrence against a charge of arson. Mr. Lawrence, a homeless man, had been living under the train trestle on the border of Peachton in Harrison County.

Last Tuesday Mr. Lawrence was seen running from the parking lot of a professional building complex on Juniper Street in Peachton. Soon after, flames were seen coming from the law offices of Minor and Henry, which were housed in the complex.

Minor and Henry!

The name Minor was some sort of connection. But Amanda still didn't see how it fit.

She continued reading.

Mr. Lawrence claimed to be rummaging through the garbage cans when he spotted the smoke. He told police officers he was running to get help.

However, police found empty gasoline canisters at his campsite under the trestle. And so the homeless man was arrested and charged with starting the fire.

How did this fit together? Amanda wondered.

Why did Chrissy have a clipping about a homeless man Amanda's father had defended?

She searched the tissue paper at the bottom of the shoe box. There were more clippings there.

But as she reached for one, she heard a car pull into the driveway. She darted to the window and peered down.

Dave and Chrissy! Back already!

Chrissy was already climbing out of the car.

Now what? Now what? Now what?

Amanda froze in panic.

She clutched the clippings to her chest. The shoe boxes were jumbled in a pile on the floor.

Now what? Now what?

She had to hide the boxes—fast!

Her heart pumping, she began pitching them frantically into the closet. When they were all in, she shut the door.

She heard the front door slam and someone start up the stairs. Chrissy was coming up to her room.

There's no way I can get out of here without running into her, Amanda realized. No way. No way. No way.

Clutching the clippings tightly in one hand, Amanda dove under the bed. She bit down on her other hand to stifle the sound of her heavy breathing as Chrissy entered the room.

"Did I leave this light on?" she heard Chrissy murmur to herself. From the movement of her feet, Amanda could tell that Chrissy was examining the room.

Amanda stifled a gasp. A clipping had fallen onto the rug. It wasn't far from Chrissy's foot.

Chrissy bent down. She picked up the clipping.

Then Amanda heard the closet door open and shut.

"Amanda?" Chrissy called, walking out of the room. Amanda listened, trying to tell from Chrissy's footsteps and voice where she was. "Amanda?" Chrissy called again. She had made her way down the hall to Amanda's room.

This is my chance, Amanda decided.

She scrambled out from under the bed and sprinted to the bedroom door.

I've got to get Mom and Dad.

I've got to show them these clippings. I've got to show them that Chrissy isn't here by accident.

She was so frightened, she couldn't think clearly.

Was it okay to leave Kyle and Merry?

They're asleep, she told herself, thinking hard, trying to figure out what to do. They're asleep. I'll be back with Mom and Dad in a few minutes. They'll be okay.

Taking a deep breath, she plunged out into the hall.

"Hey—" Chrissy called angrily. "What were you doing in there? Hey!"

But Amanda turned and ran down the stairs.

A few seconds later she was out the front door.

"Dave!" she cried. "You're still here!"

"When we got to town, Chrissy changed her mind," Dave said, standing on the front lawn. "She didn't want to see the movie, so—"

"Dave—let's go!" Amanda cried. "Hurry! Drive me to my parents! At the Beachside Inn!"

Dave hesitated for only a second. Then he ran with Amanda to the car. His tires squealed as the car peeled out of the driveway.

"I—I have the clippings," Amanda stammered. "I have to show them to my parents. I—"

She stopped as one of the clippings caught her eye.

Suddenly she grabbed hold of Dave's arm. "Dave, listen to this!"

She read the news story to him:

Arthur Lawrence, a homeless person, was acquitted today of arson charges in the Minor and Henry law office fire last Tuesday.

Mr. Lawrence's attorney, Public Defender Robert Conklin, has asked that Anton Minor of Peachton be charged with the crime.

"You've lost me," Dave confessed, his eyes straight ahead as the car bounced over the narrow, curving road.

"Don't you see?" Amanda cried, finally putting some of the pieces together. This guy, Anton Minor —he must be related to Chrissy. Maybe he's her father. Yes! He *must* be her father. Because the other clipping said he was Lilith's father."

"So he's Chrissy's and Lilith's father?" Dave asked.

"Right!" Amanda replied, thinking hard. "And my dad had him charged with setting fire to his own office!"

Dave nodded. "I follow you so far. Chrissy has a grudge against your dad because he pressed charges against her father. But that doesn't explain how she can do all those weird things."

Amanda struggled to read the clippings in the dim light. "You're right. I have no idea how Chrissy's strange powers fit into this."

"But wait," Dave continued. "Didn't you tell me Anton Minor accidentally killed himself and his wife? And that Lilith was in a coma? I still don't see what that has to do with Chrissy—"

"Whoa! I don't *believe* it!" Amanda cried.

"Huh? What?" Dave demanded.

Amanda turned to him, an expression of shock on her face. "Chrissy *is* Lilith Minor!" she said.

chapter

17

Car Trouble

"**L**ook! The photo with this clipping!" Amanda cried, waving the strip of newspaper. "It says it's Lilith. But it's Chrissy!"

"Let me see that," Dave said eagerly. He stopped the car and turned on the interior light.

"Wow, that's Chrissy all right!" he exclaimed, grabbing the clipping from Amanda. But then Dave's expression changed. "Wait. Didn't you tell me they were twins?"

"Oh. Right." Amanda's face fell. "How could I have forgotten? But look at this picture. I've seen Chrissy wear that same white dress. She had it on tonight."

"Twins dress alike sometimes," Dave reminded her. "Or maybe Chrissy has her sister's clothes."

Amanda covered her face with her hands. "I'm totally losing it. I'm not thinking straight at all!"

Gently Dave took her hands away from her face. "Stay cool. It's going to be all right. You've got this thing almost figured out. Whatever Chrissy is up to, her game is about to end."

Amanda suddenly remembered how the first clipping had burst into flames. Could Chrissy do that again?

Clutching the clippings tightly, she urged Dave to go on. "I have to show these clippings to my parents—before something happens to them."

"I hear you. Let's hurry to the Beachside Inn right now." he said.

"But what if they planned to leave there? You know. Go to a restaurant or something," Amanda fretted. "Maybe I should call. Tell them I'm coming."

Dave's expression turned thoughtful. "There's a phone booth on Channings Bluff. You can call from there."

"Okay. Hurry."

Dave lowered his foot to the gas, and the car squealed away. Amanda hung on to the seat as he swung around the curves.

A heavy fog rolled up from the ocean. It drifted across the road, making it hard to see.

Every few seconds Amanda checked the clippings in her lap to be sure they were safe. Please be okay, Merry and Kyle, she prayed silently. Please be okay.

The Mustang raced into the empty parking lot at Channings Bluff. "Wow! It's like we drove into a cloud!" Amanda exclaimed, watching the blanket of thick white mist swirl around the car.

One streetlight cast a hazy glow over the dark parking lot.

Dave pulled up next to the phone booth. "Do you have a quarter for the phone?" Amanda asked.

Dave didn't answer. He stared straight ahead.

"Dave, what's wrong?" Amanda asked. "Do you see something out there?"

Slowly Dave began to sway. His head and upper body moved slowly in a circle. His eyes were wide, as if he were in some kind of trance.

"Dave?" Amanda cried, pounding his shoulder. "Dave—why are you doing that? Stop! Stop it— please!"

Dave continued to sway, his expression blank, his eyes unblinking.

"Dave—please! Please!" Amanda shrieked help-lessly.

Suddenly Dave pitched forward.

His forehead slammed hard against the steering wheel.

"Dave!" Amanda screamed.

She cradled his head in her hands and tried to pull him up.

But when she saw his face, she let go.

Blood spurted from his nose and mouth. And it flowed from his ears.

His head fell back, and he stared at her with wide, lifeless eyes.

Suzi! Amanda thought. Just like Suzi!

What can I do? What? I can't let him bleed to death!

Fighting back her panic, Amanda pushed him forward. Reached into his pocket. Tugged out his wallet.

"Quarter, quarter, quarter," she murmured. She fumbled with the zipper of the change compartment, her hand shaking violently.

"Yes!" she cried aloud, gripping a quarter tightly.

Desperately she pushed the car door.

It wouldn't open.

Was it locked?

No.

Leaning across Dave's limp body, she tried his door.

Stuck!

She tried her door again. And again.

It wouldn't budge.

Got to get out. Got to get out.

The words repeated like a frantic chant.

She searched for something to break the window glass.

With a trembling hand she popped open the glove compartment.

A screwdriver!

With all her strength she began hacking at the glass with the sharp edge.

"Ahh!" she screamed in frustration as she

pounded away. In the movies it always looked so simple to break glass!

"Come on, Amanda, try harder!" She threw her arm into it. Again. Again.

Finally a spiderlike crack fanned out from where she'd hit. "Okay!" The window was giving way.

Gasping with each lunge, Amanda hacked at the cracked window glass.

"Nooooo!" She stopped and uttered a low cry as a face suddenly leered in at her from outside.

Chrissy!

chapter

18

"Sorry, Amanda!"

"Chrissy—how?" Amanda managed to choke out.

The car doors all flew open as if a powerful wind gust had snapped them back.

With a cry of terror, Amanda fell onto Dave's limp body. His head bobbed lifelessly against the steering wheel.

"Oh, Dave!" Amanda sobbed, frantically pulling herself off him.

In the swirling fog, the light glancing off her hair, Chrissy floated like a pale, unearthly ghost. She laughed, a raspy, joyless laugh. "Might as well come out, Amanda," she called in a teasing singsong. "You can't get away from me."

Amanda tried to sink lower into the seat. But there was nowhere to hide, no way to escape.

Chrissy's eerily pale face drew close. "Come out! Come out!" she sang in her frightening, singsong voice.

Desperate to get away, Amanda tumbled into the backseat.

And then a powerful force, strong as a hurricane, began pushing her. Pushing her forward.

"No!" she shouted, digging her fingers into the car seat. "No!" She pushed back until her fingers ached.

Then, with tremendous force, Amanda felt herself being hurled toward the open door. She toppled out of the car. Onto her hands and knees.

And the force—like an invisible hand—pushed even harder.

Slid her across the pavement. Through the cold, wet fog.

Sliding. Sliding so fast and hard.

And then lifting her up. Up. Face-to-face with a grinning Chrissy.

"What do you want? How are you doing these things? Why?" Amanda demanded breathlessly, pushing her dark curls out of her eyes.

Surrounded by dark fog, Chrissy floated up onto the hood of the Mustang, her long legs dangling. With her head cocked to the side, she studied Amanda a moment before speaking. "You know, they say people use only a small portion of their brains. Well, I use all of my brain. I can do anything. Anything!"

As if to demonstrate, Chrissy floated off the car

hood, hovering a few inches above it. "Impressive?" She laughed.

I don't believe this, Amanda thought weakly.

So I *did* see her float.

"Why are you trying to hurt us?" she blurted out.

"Why?" Chrissy echoed bitterly. "That's easy. Real easy. Do you know why my father killed himself? Because of *your* father!"

"But your father didn't kill himself," Amanda protested. "You told me your family was in an accident."

"My father wasn't a man who had accidents," Chrissy replied, sneering. "My father was a great man. A genius. But your father hounded him. Had him arrested. Ruined his life. Ruined all of our lives. Mom's and Lilith's too. Poor Lilith. And so my father tried to spare us. He tried to spare us by ending our lives."

"My father was only doing his job," Amanda insisted in a trembling voice. "If that homeless man was innocent—"

"Who cares?" Chrissy shrieked. "My father's life was worth much more than his. You can't even compare the two. Mediocre little people like your father are jealous of brilliant people. They love to destroy the truly great men like my father!"

"What happened to those families you gave as references?" Amanda demanded.

"Who? The judge and the assistant D.A.? They got only what they deserved," Chrissy replied cruelly. "And now it's your family's turn."

Chrissy slid off the car and began moving through the fog toward Amanda.

Run! Amanda commanded herself.

Get away! Now!

But her legs felt as heavy as stone.

"Let me go! You can't do this to me!" she pleaded. "It—it's not fair."

"Fair?" Chrissy shrieked. "It's *totally* fair, Amanda. My mother, my father, my sister—my whole family is gone. And now your family will be gone."

"But—but—" Amanda sputtered, thinking hard. "Imagine what you could do with your powers," she cried desperately. "Why waste your time on us? With your powers, you could get rich!"

Chrissy didn't reply. She raised her arms, and a cold wind whipped around Amanda.

Amanda screamed as her feet were lifted off the ground.

"Stop!" Amanda pleaded as the icy wind tossed her around in the air.

She flailed her arms, trying to catch her balance.

But the powerful wind hurtled her toward the car.

Screaming into the roar of the wind, Amanda covered her head, prepared to smash into the fender.

"Ohhh!"

She was pushed into the car.

She landed hard in the passenger seat beside Dave's lifeless body.

The doors slammed shut.

The locks clicked.

Through the windows Amanda saw Chrissy laughing. Enjoying her triumph.

Amanda struggled to move, to break out.

But a force held her in place.

She stared in helpless horror as the emergency brake released. The engine started.

"Sorry, Amanda!" was Chrissy's taunting call. "You lose!"

The car raced forward.

Through the split-rail fence.

And over the steep bluff.

chapter

19

Swallowed Up

Down into the blackness.

Amanda curled into a tight ball, covering her head.

And waited for the crash.

The car hit hard, then bounced. She cried out as her head hit the ceiling.

Then the car pitched forward. She fell over Dave's bouncing body, then felt herself being jolted again, slammed hard against the passenger door. So hard she felt her breath pour out in a long *whoosh*.

The car rocked, then steadied itself.

Gasping, struggling to draw air into her aching lungs, Amanda peered out into the darkness.

I'm alive, she thought, dazed.

I'm alive. Somehow, I'm still alive.

But how?

She tried the passenger door. It was jammed shut.

Amanda stared at Dave and fought back her tears. Poor Dave. She had to do something—fast.

Reaching over Dave's body, she rattled the driver's door. And pushed it open.

She stared down at the black, churning ocean thirty feet beneath her. As her eyes adjusted to the darkness, she could see the white foaming lines of surf. And she could hear the soft roar of the waves.

Why hadn't the car dropped into the ocean? she wondered, staring out, her heart still thudding in her chest.

And then she remembered the boulders that Dave had pointed out to her. The three dark boulders that jutted out from the side of the bluff.

The car had become wedged on them.

But for how long?

The car shifted as some of the rock crumbled under its weight.

I have to get out, Amanda realized. She peered down through the open car door. It was a long way down to the water.

She felt Dave's chest. No heartbeat. He was dead.

The car shifted again. Amanda tumbled forward.

Maybe I can lower myself onto the top of that boulder, she thought, staring down at it desperately.

The cracking rock made the car shift again.

Amanda could see that it was about to topple

into the ocean. Grabbing the open door, she pulled herself over Dave, slid out—and let go.

She hit rock and fell hard onto her shoulder and side. As the wave of pain rolled over her, she heard a loud cracking sound.

Then, staring into the darkness, she watched the car fall end over end down the remainder of the bluff. It hit the water nose first, with a sickening *splat*. Splashing water and crunching metal echoing over the steady rush of the waves.

Amanda raised her eyes to the top of the bluff. Was Chrissy still up there? Had Chrissy seen that Amanda had escaped from the car?

She swung her legs around and started crawling to the far side of the boulder, peering down below her.

She let out a shrill scream as she saw the enormous eye staring at her.

And then Amanda started to slip off the boulder. She almost lost her grip as the gigantic face moved toward her, its gaping mouth open wide as if to swallow her whole.

chapter

20

Chrissy Takes Charge

Amanda clawed at the rock, struggling to regain her grip.

"Chrissy! No!" she shrieked. Chrissy had used her powers to turn herself into a hideous giant.

And then—as she found her balance and pulled herself back onto the boulder top, Amanda saw that she was wrong.

It's not Chrissy, she scolded herself. It's one of the faces Dave's brother and his friends painted on the rocks.

She let out her breath slowly.

Slowly, painfully, she groped for footholds in the rock to lower herself to the beach. The fog made it almost impossible to see.

It seemed to take hours to climb down.

Finally she stepped onto the beach and stared back up at the side of the bluff.

The fog grew thicker. The dark bluff appeared to be rolling over her.

And then Amanda felt her knees buckle and her legs slip out from under her.

She struggled to remain upright. But she was sinking now, sinking onto the cool, wet sand, sinking into the gentle darkness.

When Amanda opened her eyes, bright sunlight made her close them again. She squinted into an intense morning brightness.

I must have passed out, she realized, slowly raising herself to her elbows. Kneeling, she brushed wet sand off the front of her T-shirt.

She scanned the narrow, rocky beach against the bluff wall. Then looked out over the ocean, searching for any sign of Dave's Mustang.

It was gone. Sunk or carried away.

Dave's handsome face flashed into her head. Her eyes brimmed with tears. It's my fault he's dead, she told herself. He died trying to help me.

No. It's Chrissy's fault.

Chrissy's taunting, evil face swept away the picture of Dave. Chrissy killed Dave, Amanda thought bitterly. And she'll kill my whole family if I don't stop her.

Raising her eyes, Amanda saw the gross, clown-ish faces painted on the boulders. They grinned their ugly grins at her. "Thanks, guys," she murmured as she climbed to her feet.

Now what? she wondered. Her ripped jeans and sneakers were soaking wet from the sand. She pulled them off and walked into the ocean in her underpants and T-shirt.

The only way she'd be able to see to the top would be to swim out. Perhaps if a tourist was peering over the scenic overlook, she could call out.

The saltwater burned her scraped knee. As she swam, her stomach growled with hunger. Several yards out, she turned, treading water, and gazed up to the top. The only evidence of what had happened was the hole in the split-rail fence.

After ten minutes of treading water, no one had appeared. Mom and Dad have to be looking for me by now, Amanda assured herself.

Of course, it wouldn't occur to them to look for me at the bottom of a sheer bluff. Not right away. But, surely, someone will spot the hole in the fence.

Amanda swam back to shore. She threw her jeans over her shoulder and slipped into her sneakers. There's no way back up that bluff, she saw. But I can probably follow the shoreline around to our house.

Every muscle in her body ached as she set out along the shore. I have to keep going, she urged herself. My family has no idea what danger they're in.

She walked for hours, trudging slowly, shielding her eyes against the burning morning sun. Up the beach. Then through the tangled woods.

At last she passed the boulders that housed Mr. Jinx's grave. A few minutes later, she climbed up to the shed near the pool.

Behind the shed, she slipped back into her jeans. Then, taking a deep breath, she stepped up onto the deck.

It's so quiet, she thought. Too quiet.

Where is everyone?

Huddling at the side of the sliding-glass doors, she peeked in. The living room stood silent and empty.

With the toe of her sneaker, Amanda slid the glass door open wide enough to allow her to slip inside. Immediately she ducked behind the long curtains to her right.

She heard a voice. From the kitchen.

Chrissy. Speaking on the telephone.

Ignoring the fear that ran down her back, Amanda listened hard.

"Don't worry, Mrs. Conklin. I agree," Chrissy was saying. "I think you're smart to look for her in Shadyside. I overheard her and her friend Dave. I'm pretty sure I heard Dave say he'd drive her to Shadyside."

How can this be? Amanda asked herself. *Has Chrissy really tricked my parents into driving to Shadyside?*

"Yes, if Amanda calls, I'll let you know right away," Chrissy was saying. "No, me neither. I have no idea why she would run off. But as you just said,

Amanda has been acting weird lately. So who knows? Right. Right."

There was a brief pause as Amanda's mother said something on the other end.

Then Chrissy finished the conversation with words that gave Amanda cold chills.

"No. Don't worry about Merry and Kyle. I'll take good care of them until you get back."

chapter

21

You Die First!

Amanda shut her eyes and leaned back against the wall.

What am I going to do? she asked herself. Mom and Dad are in Shadyside. And Kyle and Merry are completely at Chrissy's mercy.

Before she had time to think, the front doorbell rang.

Peeking out from behind the curtains, she saw a dark-uniformed police officer at the front door. "Are the Conklins in?" he asked Chrissy.

"Not at the moment," Chrissy replied sweetly. "They're out looking for their daughter, the one who was reported missing last night. She still hasn't come home. Is there any news about Amanda?"

"Well, we're not sure," the policeman replied. "Some vehicle crashed through the fence at the overlook. Could Amanda Conklin have been in a car?"

"I don't know," Chrissy told him. "She was out with her boyfriend."

"Dave Malone?" the sheriff questioned.

Chrissy cocked her head thoughtfully. "Yeah."

"His parents told us he was driving a blue 1978 Mustang," the officer revealed. "Somebody hit that fence, but there's no sign of the vehicle. It will be a while before we can get a boat up here to dredge for it below the cliff."

"Dredge!" Chrissy cried, pretending to be horrified.

The sheriff nodded. "It's very deep below that bluff. A vehicle might have gone right under."

"Oh, I hope not!" Chrissy gasped.

The officer muttered agreement. Then he said, "We don't usually begin a search for missing persons until they've been gone for forty-eight hours. But with this crashed fence and all—I don't know. We'll see."

Chrissy leaned confidentially toward the man. "This is just my opinion, of course, but I think she and this boy may have gone off somewhere together. She was really crazy about him and she's been having problems at home lately. You know, not getting along with her parents."

"Thanks for the information, miss," said the officer. "I'll keep it in mind. I hope that's all it is."

"Yes, officer. I hope so too," said Chrissy.

"Thanks for coming by. I'll tell the Conklins when they call."

After Chrissy shut the door, she picked up a towel and headed out of the living room toward the bathroom.

Slipping out from behind the curtains, Amanda silently made her way up to her room. She could hear the shower running in the bathroom. As she entered her bedroom, the calico kitten jumped up onto the bed.

Amanda lifted the kitten into her arms. "Hey, smart kitty," she said softly. "Keeping out of trouble? Keeping away from Chrissy?"

The kitten meowed plaintively in her hands.

"You must be hungry. But I can't do much for you now," Amanda told the kitten as she petted her. "At least I can set you free so Chrissy won't get you."

She sneaked down the stairs and out of the house. Then she set the kitten on the ground. But the kitten wouldn't leave her. "Go away! Shoo!" Amanda whispered, but the kitten stayed and rubbed against her ankles.

Amanda wasn't sure how to keep Merry and Kyle safe. Chrissy was so powerful. How could she beat her?

Amanda's stomach growled. She felt dizzy, faint with hunger.

Maybe I can get to the kitchen without being seen.

As quietly as she could, she slid open the door.

She made a quick dash for the kitchen, silently shutting the door behind her. Immediately her eyes lit on a box of Cheerios on the counter.

Ripping it open, she stuffed a handful of cereal into her mouth. No food had ever tasted so wonderful to her. Opening the refrigerator, she grabbed a carton of orange juice and downed it, letting the juice spill out the sides of the container.

With food in her stomach, Amanda felt her head clear. This is my chance to get Merry and Kyle out of here. Why hasn't Chrissy hurt them yet? she wondered.

Maybe she's waiting for a way to make it look like an accident.

Maybe she wants to get my parents out of the way first. That way they won't be around to protect them. I know she'll get to them eventually. She said she was going to destroy our entire family.

But when? How much time do I have?

Amanda ran down the hall to Merry and Kyle's room. Their beds were empty and unmade.

Where were they so early in the morning? What had Chrissy done with them?

A wave of cold fear swept over her. She sank back against the door.

Down the hall, the shower turned off.

Amanda ducked behind the kids' door. Through the opening between the hinges, she saw Chrissy step out of the bathroom wrapped in a towel. She disappeared into her room.

Taking a deep breath, Amanda crept down the hall past Chrissy's closed door. Down the stairs, moving as silently as possible.

At the bottom of the stairs, she remembered she'd left the Cheerios open on the kitchen counter. The open box would tip Chrissy off.

Suddenly the front door opened. Startled, Amanda leapt into the living room behind the couch and dropped to her hands and knees.

"Chrissy, we've got them!" a familiar voice called brightly. Kyle.

"We found the inner tubes," Merry called.

Amanda let out a long, relieved sigh. They were both all right—for now.

Chrissy came down the stairs dressed in a hot pink tank suit. "Okay, you guys, into the kitchen for breakfast," she ordered them.

Amanda knew there was nothing she could do just then. As she slipped out through the front door, she heard Chrissy ask, "Who left this cereal open?"

"Not me," said Kyle.

Amanda circled the house and tore into the woods. Her instinct told her to run as far and fast as she could.

She raced between the shimmering trees, pounding out onto the beach. From there she kept running down the shore.

As she ran, her temples began to throb. She slowed down, then stopped, clutching her forehead.

"Hey!" Amanda cried out when she heard a voice in her head.

A clear, cold voice.

Chrissy's voice! ~

You were here, weren't you, Amanda? You're not dead after all.

The voice pounded in Amanda's head like a heavy stone hammer. She grasped her forehead as if to keep it from exploding from the pain.

Amanda you must die first—then Merry and Kyle!

"Are you all right, miss?"

Amanda turned quickly and faced a middle-aged, balding man who had been dragging a wave-runner across the ocean toward the shore. "Are you sick?" he asked.

"Uh—my head," Amanda mumbled. "Head-ache."

"I have some aspirin in my pack on my blanket over there. Would you like some?" the man offered.

Anything that might help the pain sounded good to Amanda. "Yes, please," she said.

"I'll be right back," the man told her.

As Amanda waited, she saw a flash of hot pink coming through the woods. Chrissy!

Amanda searched around desperately.

You first! You first! The words thundered in her head.

That's it, Amanda realized. That's how I can protect Merry and Kyle. They'll be safe as long as I stay alive!

Chrissy was floating closer. Closer!

Amanda's eyes settled on the man's wave-runner.

Without hesitating, she ran to it, pulling it into the surf.

"Hey!" the man cried, running toward her. "Hey!"

Amanda moved fast. She turned the ignition and jumped on. A second later she roared away from shore.

Thanks for teaching me to ride this thing, Dave, Amanda thought as she held tight to the handlebars.

Thinking of Dave reminded Amanda of his island. It was stocked with food. The perfect place to hide.

And it's full of weapons! she remembered.

Amanda leaned her weight to the right and headed out in the direction of the island. She realized she could get her bearings by watching the shore.

At the Beachside Inn she headed straight out toward the island.

Before long, the tangled underbrush and scrubby trees of Dave's island came into view. It gave Amanda new hope.

She pulled onto the narrow beach and cut the engine. Struggling under its weight, Amanda pushed the wave-runner up the beach and into the bushes.

Then she stepped away and gazed at the back end of the wave-runner peeking out from the bushes.

Better cover it with some branches just to be on the safe side, she decided. She began to snap off some pine branches, when a searing pain shot across her forehead.

The pain made her cry out. It made the trees spin all around her.

She dropped to her knees in the sand.

Merry and Kyle are mine! came Chrissy's voice inside her head. *They're mine, Amanda! Mine!*

chapter

22

One More Shock

Amanda let herself into the shed. She grabbed the first white box she saw, and ripped it open. It was a bag of dehydrated banana chips. She tossed handfuls of them into her mouth without even tasting them.

Then she stepped out of her jeans, which were soaked from her ride on the wave-runner. As she hung them over the chair, her eyes traveled around the shed.

She gazed at the spot where Dave had kissed her—the soft, warm kiss that would never happen again.

She could feel tears forming in her eyes.

No time, she told herself. No time for tears.

She forced Dave from her mind.

The knife! She remembered the knife he'd

handed her. There had been other knives here. Amanda began searching around the shed.

In a low wooden cabinet she found a long knife with a dangerous-looking hook at the end of the blade. It was sheathed in a leather pouch attached to leather ties.

Amanda removed the glistening knife from the pouch and hacked off the legs of her wet jeans. These will just weigh me down on the ride back, she told herself.

She slipped into her new shorts and tied the knife pouch to the belt loops. Then she began rummaging through the boxes and trunks for anything that might be useful.

"Hey!" Amanda cried out as she felt her feet lift off the ground. She hurtled over the trunk—as if an invisible hand had shoved her.

Amanda screamed and crashed into a cabinet, sending a clay pot smashing to the ground.

Amanda, Chrissy's voice burst into her head as once again the pain began to shoot along her forehead like an electric current. *I haven't forgotten about you.*

Amanda jammed the heels of her hands into her forehead. She shut her eyes tight and ground her back teeth in a fierce effort to block Chrissy out.

You're not as close as you were before, are you? Chrissy's voice continued. *I can tell, but I can find you. But not now. I have something more important to attend to right now. Come here, Merry!*

Amanda's eyes snapped open wide.

The pain vanished. The voice disappeared.

"What's happening?" Amanda cried. She raced out of the shed and through the bushes back to the wave-runner. Frantically she shoved the wave-runner back into the water.

"I'm coming, Merry! Hang on!" she cried desperately as she zoomed back across the water to the summerhouse.

Amanda neared the beach area in time to see Chrissy at the back of the engine-powered skiff that came with the house. Merry and Kyle weren't with her. Chrissy was heading out to sea, in the direction of Dave's island.

Then, to her horror, Amanda saw Kyle stick his head up. He had something stuffed in his mouth. Chrissy spoke sharply and his head disappeared back down.

Merry *had* to be beside him, Amanda realized. What was Chrissy going to do to them?

Amanda opened the throttle hard, pushing the wave-runner to its limit.

Hang on! she told herself. Hang on!

Twenty yards from the skiff, Amanda saw that Chrissy had spotted her. Instantly a line of pain seared Amanda's forehead.

As she cried out, the wave-runner tilted dangerously to the left.

"No, you don't!" Amanda shouted furiously, righting herself by shifting her weight hard in the opposite direction.

Closer. Closer to the skiff.

"Ow!" Amanda screamed as Chrissy threw another crushing headache at her.

But she gritted her teeth and squeezed down on the handles of the wave-runner.

"Ohhh!" The pain suddenly became so unbearable that Amanda had to shut her eyes.

When she forced them open, she saw to her surprise that the skiff was spinning in a crazy zigzag pattern.

Chrissy has lost control of it, Amanda realized.

She can't make a mind connection *and* pay attention to what she's doing at the same time.

As Chrissy returned her attention to controlling the skiff, Amanda's headache evaporated. She moved in closer, gripping the handlebars as she roared over the tossing waters. Just ten yards from the skiff now.

Merry's head popped up from the bottom of the skiff. She was also gagged and her eyes were red with tears. Kyle raised himself up next to her. Chrissy yelled at them and they ducked down out of sight again.

Closer. Amanda moved in closer.

Chrissy fixed her in a steely gaze. Then she lifted both arms to the sky, reaching as if she were trying to touch the white clouds with her fingertips.

What is she doing? Amanda wondered. What is she trying to pull now?

She didn't have to wait long to find out.

As Chrissy slowly lowered her arms, a blazing

yellow-white line of jagged electricity shot out of her hands.

Amanda heard the crackle—then felt a hard jolt as the white-hot current shot through the wave-runner.

The wave-runner fell out from under her.

Jerking and twisting in pain, Amanda flew into the current, into the crackling, sparking air, into the jagged, sharp, cutting flash of pure power.

And then plummeted down into the churning waters to drown.

chapter

23

Cut!

*I*nto the inky water.

The electrical pain still shooting through her body. The cold shock of the water bringing its own agony.

Drowning. I'm drowning, she realized.

And saw the faces of her brother and sister.

Their pretty faces. Their wide, innocent eyes.

No!

And decided she couldn't drown.

Up now. Ignoring the pain, she forced herself up.

To the surface. A gasp of air. Another.

"Ow!" New pain as she rapped her head on something hard. It's the skiff! It's above me!

She knew what she had to do. Reaching up with both hands, she grabbed hold of the side—and hoisted herself up into the skiff.

As Amanda shook water from her eyes, Chrissy reacted fast. She grabbed Merry, who was tied as well as gagged. Merry cried and squirmed frantically. Her entire body quivered in terror.

Chrissy held Merry tightly. Amanda could see the nails of one of Chrissy's hands digging into Merry's arm.

Chrissy's free hand came up with a knife, the long skinning knife Amanda had put in Chrissy's drawer.

With a flash of silver, Chrissy cut the air with the knife—then held it to Merry's throat. "This is for my father!" Chrissy screamed.

chapter

24

Chrissy Flies a Kite

Desperate, Amanda hurled herself across the skiff.

She tackled Chrissy around the waist, burying her head hard into Chrissy's midsection.

The skiff pitched dangerously from side to side.

Chrissy stumbled back, gasping for breath.

Merry rolled away from her.

The knife clattered to the floor of the boat. Amanda kicked it to the back. Then she grabbed hold of Chrissy's hair and yanked her head back hard.

Chrissy shot her hand up, hitting Amanda squarely under the chin with the heel of her hand.

The blow sent Amanda stumbling backward on top of Kyle.

Before Amanda could struggle to her feet, Chrissy rose above her. She narrowed her eyes and glared furiously at Amanda.

Once again Amanda felt a cold wind, an overpowering force.

She flailed her arms. She tried to kick.

But she was helpless against this frozen hurricane.

It lifted her up, up out of the skiff, into the frigid, swirling air.

Like a kite, she thought. Helpless as a kite in a windstorm.

"The higher they go, the harder they fall!" Chrissy called up to her, her eyes blazing as they held Amanda in their evil grip.

And as Chrissy's laughter rang out over the roar of the wind, Amanda came slamming down.

Sinking down. Down into the throbbing pain.

Down into the boat.

Where she spun around and made a desperate grab for Chrissy's ankle.

"Let go!" Chrissy shrieked, pulling away.

Somehow Amanda held on.

"I guess you want more," Chrissy threatened. "All right. You asked for it!"

Still clutching Chrissy's ankle, Amanda braced for more pain.

But to her surprise, the boat jolted forward and Chrissy's ankle jerked out of her hand.

Chrissy seemed to disappear.

Confused, Amanda raised her eyes—and saw Chrissy, her mouth open wide, flying backward through the air.

chapter

25

A Sinking Feeling

Amanda gaped as Chrissy spun higher into the air. Chrissy waved her arms helplessly. Then her arms shot straight up and she plummeted downward. Her head hit the bow of the boat with a sickening *crack*.

Pushing her drenched hair from her eyes, Amanda dragged herself to her knees. She stared hard at Chrissy, expecting her to get up.

But Chrissy lay sprawled on her back, her head tilted at an odd angle, her eyes shut.

It took Amanda another moment to figure out what had happened. When Chrissy's ankle had jerked out of Amanda's hand, the boat had crashed into a boulder poking up out of the water. The crash had sent Chrissy flying.

Behind Amanda, the motor sent up a cloud of dark smoke. Then it coughed and conked out.

Silence.

Amanda could hear her own pounding heart over the steady, rhythmic wash of the waves.

Struggling to catch her breath, she crawled over to her brother and sister, who were sitting near the stern. Grabbing the knife that Chrissy had threatened Merry with, Amanda cut their ropes in quick, frantic motions.

Merry burst into loud sobs and reached out with both hands for Amanda. Kyle sat up, dazed, his eyes darting wildly.

Amanda wrapped Merry in a hug. "Kyle, are you okay?" she asked.

He gazed back at her blankly and didn't answer.

"Where was Chrissy taking you?" Amanda asked Kyle.

He stared back at her, confusion on his face. "An island," he said finally.

She was bringing them to Dave's island, Amanda told herself. She was going to kill us on the island, where we wouldn't be found.

Feeling a cold shiver run down her back, Amanda grabbed up the ropes that had bound Merry and Kyle. She tugged Chrissy by the feet, pulling her closer. Then she hurriedly began tying up her arms and legs, knotting and double-knotting the ropes.

I should push her over the side, Amanda thought

bitterly. I should push her over and watch her drown.

But I can't. I'm not a murderer.

"We'll take her back to the house and call the police," she told Kyle.

He gazed back at her blankly. He opened his mouth, but no words came out. Merry clung to Amanda's arm, sobbing loudly, afraid to let go.

"We've got to push the boat off the rock," Amanda said, crawling to the bow. She climbed out onto the wet, slippery boulder and pushed.

The skiff didn't budge.

She lowered her shoulder against it and pushed again.

With a creak and a groan, the boat floated free.

Amanda hopped back in and made her way to the motor. A hard tug of the rope started it right up.

She hugged Merry with one hand and tried to turn the skiff around with the other. She had headed them toward shore, when Kyle's voice rose over the motor's roar.

"Water!" Kyle cried in a tight, shrill voice. "Water!"

Amanda turned to see water flowing into the boat from a hole poked in the bow. "Quick—Kyle! That bucket!" she cried, pointing. "Grab it! Bail out the water! Hurry!"

He stared back at her blankly.

"Kyle—are you okay?" Amanda demanded, feeling dread knot her stomach. "Kyle? Get the bucket—*please!*"

He shook his head as if he didn't understand.

Water splashed into the boat. Amanda saw that it was already two inches deep.

She turned to see the beach come into view.

We're so close! she thought. So close!

"Kyle—please—bail out water!"

He took a step toward the bucket, then stopped, still shaking his head.

Water spilled into the boat faster.

Amanda could feel the boat drop in the water.

"We're *th*inking!" Merry lisped, tears running down her red cheeks. Amanda held her against her chest, trying to comfort her.

She made her way over to the bucket. But she could see it was too late.

The boat dipped. The motor sputtered.

We're sinking, Amanda realized to her horror.

We're all going to drown.

chapter

26

Chrissy Wins

*F*rantically Amanda hoisted the bucket and started to shovel out the water.

But it was too late.

The boat sank deeper. The motor died.

We're going under, she realized.

And then a desperate thought burst into her head: Maybe I can jump out, swim alongside, and pull the boat to shore.

She didn't have time to think about it. She set Merry down. Then took a deep breath and plunged over the side.

To Amanda's shock, her body scraped the sandy bottom.

"Hey!" she cried out as she lowered her feet. "Hey, it's shallow!"

Her heart pounded. She felt like cheering. "Kyle, you can walk to shore! It's shallow here!"

He stared at her, narrowing his eyes in confusion.

Poor Kyle, Amanda thought. He's in shock, I guess.

She reached over the side of the boat, grabbed his hands, and helped him into the water. It came up to his shoulders, but he was able to walk.

Merry jumped into Amanda's arms as the skiff sank even lower.

What about Chrissy? Amanda thought. She stared at Chrissy, still sprawled on her back, half floating in the invading water, breathing noisily through her open mouth.

Can I leave her here to drown? Amanda asked herself.

The answer was no.

"Kyle, I need you to hold on to your sister," Amanda instructed him. As soon as the water was waist-deep, she handed Merry to Kyle. Then Amanda turned back to the sinking skiff and grabbed Chrissy by the hair. The boat made a loud gurgling sound as it plunged underwater. Chrissy floated free. Amanda wrapped her arm around Chrissy's waist and dragged her to shore.

The house was empty and silent. Exhausted and soaked, Amanda and Kyle had dragged Chrissy all the way up to the house. Then Amanda pulled her into the living room and dropped her onto the carpet.

Chrissy hadn't stirred or shown any signs of waking up. A large wound on the back of her head was still wet with dark blood.

"I—I'm going to call the police," Amanda managed to choke out, hunched over, gasping for air. "Don't move. Just stay right there," she told Kyle and Merry.

She hurried into the kitchen. Her chest was heaving. The police number was taped to the wall next to the phone. She grabbed up the phone receiver and had started to punch in the numbers—when Kyle's terrified scream interrupted her.

"She's awake! She's awake!"

"Ohhh." Amanda let out a low groan. The phone receiver fell out of her hand. She spun away and lurched back into the living room.

Chrissy was sitting up. The ropes Amanda had tied around her were popping off one by one.

Kyle and Merry had their backs pressed against the glass door. Their eyes wide with horror.

"Out! Get out!" Amanda screamed at Kyle.

Obediently Kyle grabbed Merry's hand. He pushed open the door, and they raced away.

"Chrissy—it's too late," Amanda said, thinking quickly. "I've already called the police. They'll be here any second."

Chrissy climbed to her feet. "It's never too late," she replied calmly. She pushed back her wet hair. Her hand jumped when she touched the open wound at the back of her head. "Ow."

"Chrissy—listen—" Amanda started, taking a step back.

"Thanks for the nap," Chrissy said casually. "It sort of recharged my batteries, if you know what I mean." An unpleasant smile formed on her face.

"Chrissy—"

"I'm sorry, Amanda," Chrissy continued, the expression in her eyes growing cold. "But it looks like I win."

chapter

27

A Fireball

Amanda felt her knees buckle.

Chrissy took a step closer, her eyes glowing as they locked onto Amanda.

I've got to get out, Amanda realized. I've got to get away from her.

"You're not moving," Chrissy said softly as if reading her thoughts. She swept her hand in front of her—and a large ceramic vase flew across the room.

Amanda let out a startled shriek as the vase hit the wall above her head and shattered into a thousand pieces.

She ducked low and made a run for the door.

But Chrissy moved quickly to block her path. Another sweep of her arm made chairs lift off the floor. Ashtrays, books, candlesticks—all began whirling crazily around the room as if caught up in an invisible cyclone.

The pictures flew off the walls and smashed against the floor. Glass shattered. Wood splintered. The whole room spun and tilted.

Amanda covered her head with both arms.

I'm trapped, she realized. Trapped. No escape.

As all of the objects whirled faster and faster around her, she edged toward the window.

"No way!" Chrissy's furious voice rose over the clatter and crashing.

Amanda opened her eyes in time to see Chrissy point to the window. With a loud *whoosh,* a line of flame ran up the side of the curtains.

"Oh!" Amanda cried out as she leaped back from the orange flames.

Whooooop whoooop whoooop!

The smoke alarm shrieked into action.

Books and flower vases hurled themselves around the room.

The flames spread quickly. Onto the walls. Onto the couch. Onto the carpet.

"Chrissy—we've got to get out! Both of us!" Amanda shouted, choking on the black smoke that swept the room.

"You're not getting away," Chrissy replied.

"But the fire—"

Through the billowing smoke, Amanda saw

Chrissy move quickly toward her, taking long, rapid strides.

Flames shot up in the center of the room. The wallpaper peeled under the scorching heat.

Chrissy moved closer, her eyes locked on Amanda's. "You're not getting away, Amanda," she repeated calmly.

Her arms outstretched, Chrissy started to dive toward Amanda.

She didn't see the calico kitten dart under her feet.

With a startled cry, Chrissy stumbled over the kitten—and fell face forward into the flames.

This is my chance! Amanda realized.

Choking on the thick, sour smoke, she bent to grab up the kitten. Then she hurtled through the spinning books and vases, through the tossing yellow flames, through the black, billowing smoke —out the door.

Still choking and gasping, she ran. Toward the shed where Merry and Kyle waited, huddled together against the wall.

A few feet from the shed Amanda turned back to the house.

And saw a huge fireball roll out the door.

"Ohhh." She uttered a hoarse cry as she saw arms inside the fireball. And legs.

And realized the fireball was Chrissy. Chrissy in flames. Chrissy raising her fiery arms to the sky.

Then sinking to the deck floor. The flames spreading across the deck. Back onto the house.

All flames now.

All burned. All finished.

The whole evil summer.

So bright. And so dark.

chapter

28

All Over

Dr. Miller leaned forward on his desk, his hands clasped. "I wanted to have a talk with you, Amanda," he said, gazing into her eyes as if searching her soul. "I wanted another chance to go over everything with you."

"Thank you," Amanda replied uncomfortably. She scratched her shoulder. "This uniform itches. The prison laundry starches it so much—"

The psychiatrist nodded. "You do understand why the police arrested you?" he asked softly.

Amanda made a disgusted face. "They were like everyone else. They didn't believe a word I said." She sighed unhappily.

"They believed that Chrissy was burned to death," Dr. Miller said, continuing to study her. "Until they found the wound on the back of her head. When they saw that, they knew that Chrissy had been hit first, before the fire. They had to assume that you killed her first. Then set the fire to make it look as if she burned to death."

"But that's a total lie!" Amanda exclaimed. "I told them how Chrissy hit her head on the boat."

"No one ever found the boat," Dr. Miller interrupted, clasping and unclasping his hands.

"It sank in the ocean," Amanda repeated for the hundredth time. "The tide must have carried it away."

"I know," the psychiatrist said. "I just wanted you to understand why the police suspected you. And when they saw you running from the fire—"

"I was running to Merry and Kyle," Amanda broke in. "But what's the point? I've told this story about a hundred times, but no one believes me." Amanda choked back a sob. "If only Kyle could speak. But, poor thing—he's in shock. He hasn't said a word since the fire."

She looked up and saw the beginnings of a smile on Dr. Miller's face. "Amanda, I have wonderful news for you. Kyle is much better. He began speaking this morning, and his story does match yours."

Those words brought a smile to Amanda's face. "That's great!"

Dr. Miller smiled too. "And that neighbor of the murdered judge—she told the police all she knew about Chrissy."

"That was the girl I talked to on the phone,"

Amanda said. "I was calling for a reference. The girl couldn't talk to me."

"She talked plenty to the police," Dr. Miller said. "And now you're being set free, Amanda. I just wanted to have this talk to make sure everything was clear."

"I—I just can't believe Chrissy is really dead!" Amanda blurted out. "She was so evil! It's still hard for me to believe she's actually gone."

"Yes, she's dead," Dr. Miller said solemnly. He raised his eyes to Amanda. "I have one more surprise for you. Maybe you've already guessed it."

"What's that?" Amanda asked.

"Her name wasn't Chrissy. Her name was Lilith."

"Huh?" Amanda reacted with surprise. "But Lilith was in a coma!" she exclaimed.

"Yes," Dr. Miller replied, nodding. "One day she was in a deep coma. The next day she had vanished from the hospital. Into thin air." He sighed. "Lilith somehow assumed strange new powers while in the coma. And she set out to get revenge for her father and mother's death."

"Weird," Amanda muttered, shaking her head thoughtfully. "So who was Chrissy? Why did Lilith take the name Chrissy?"

"Well," Dr. Miller replied, scratching the back of his head, "we don't really know why she took that name. According to a family photo album we found, Chrissy was the name of her cat."

* * *

It seemed as if the hugging would never stop. Merry and Kyle clung to Amanda as if they hadn't seen her in years! Everyone cried and laughed and cried some more.

What a reunion!

And then her parents apologized again and again for not believing her. And when the apologizing stopped, the hugging and crying and laughing started all over again.

It felt so good to Amanda to be out in the sunshine, to breathe the warm, fresh air. To dress in her own clothes again. To laugh and talk and be with the ones she loved.

Finally they all climbed into their station wagon and began the journey home.

Amanda sat in the back with Merry and Kyle, petting the calico kitten on her lap. "What a horrible time," she said sadly. "I'll be having nightmares for the rest of my life."

"Just keep telling yourself that it's over," her mother told her. "It's all over."

The kitten purred softly in Amanda's lap.

The station wagon rumbled over the narrow beach road. Amanda glanced back in time to see the remains of their summer house, black and charred, as it rolled past on the right.

And who was that girl standing in the driveway?

The girl in the white sundress, her blond hair gleaming in the sunlight? The girl with one hand raised over her head, waving to them as they drove past?

"Hey, Mom—Dad—" Amanda cried breathlessly.

But when she turned back, the girl was gone.

About the Author

"Where do you get your ideas?"

That's the question that R. L. Stine is asked most often. "I don't know where my ideas come from," he says. "But I do know that I have a lot more scary stories in my mind that I can't wait to write."

So far, he has written more than fifty mysteries and thrillers for young people, all of them bestsellers.

Bob grew up in Columbus, Ohio. Today he lives in an apartment near Central Park in New York City with his wife, Jane, and fourteen-year-old son, Matt.

THE NIGHTMARES
NEVER END . . .
WHEN YOU VISIT
FEAR STREET®

Next: *99 FEAR STREET*

A Three-part FEAR STREET Miniseries

Long ago Simon Fear kept a secret graveyard—on what is now Fear Street—for the victims of his evil. The dark, wooded lot remained untouched for almost 100 years, until the lot was cleared and a house was built. But Simon Fear's evil could not be contained. That evil rose up through the house until its dank presence seeped from the floorboards and the walls. The address is 99 Fear Street.

Coming in August 1994

THE FIRST HORROR: It begins when twin sisters, Cally and Kody Frasier, move into the house with their family. There's soon no question that the house is haunted. But the evil in the house wants to do more than just scare the family. It's going to scare them to *death!*

Coming in September 1994

THE SECOND HORROR: The evil continues when Brandt McCloy and his family move into the house. An evil ghost haunts the house now and will do anything—no matter how horrible or gruesome—to make sure Brandt does not make it out of 99 Fear Street alive.

Coming in October 1994

THE THIRD HORROR: The story of the evil house has been sold to the movies. Kody Frazier is to star, and the movie is being shot at the actual location of the evil—99 Fear Street. But if the ghost has its way, the actors in this horror film will experience *true* horror beyond their wildest dreams!

R.L. Stine